When the Mirror Breaks

A Collection of 13 Sinister
and Supernatural Stories

by Decker Schutt

When the Mirror Breaks: Vol. 1
Copyright © 2013 **Spilled the Inc**.
in conjunction with **Whiskey Creek Press**

Library of Congress is a really cool place.

Book design by Internet Theft Services, LLC
Cover design by Alex Saskalidis aka 187designz
Contributing editor: Christine Hardy

www.Brainsnorts.com

My mirror was broken long ago. I've been trying to glue the pieces back together, but it has not been easy. I would have given up many years back, so this is to those who have helped keep things together. I know you'd rather go unnamed, and I respect that as much as I respect you, and hopefully you still respect me too.

Table of Contents

<u>Preface</u>

The theme of this collection is basically "bad luck." Sometimes bad things happen to good people. Sometimes good people are desperate enough to make bad choices. Sometimes people get what they deserve. And sometimes, superstitions seem to make sense. Of course, good short stories usually have a bit of a *twist*, something to make you rethink what you just read. There are a few of those too.

Before each story is a paragraph explaining what I experienced that caused or inspired me to write that story. Some of them were just "what if?" moments, and others were things that I had seen and then twisted or played with a little bit before beginning to write. I tried not to give away too much information so as not to take too much away from your enjoyment. Hopefully, you'll agree.

1. What Is Written

*I had a vision of a boy walking through
complete darkness and finding an old man
sitting at a desk. In my vision, the boy had
no clue where he was. The man knew why
the boy was there but did not want to tell
him. I sat down to type from about midnight
until 3 in the morning, continuously, start to
finish. I had never written anything in such
a way, and that uniqueness is why this is the
first story in the book. I think writing at that
time of night, mentally tired, and in similar
darkness, helped the story "feel" a certain
way. I hope you agree.*

A boy walked down a dark hallway towards a dot of
light that looked far enough way that it might take an
hour for him to reach it. He was very surprised as it
grew far more quickly than he expected, although he
wasn't really sure just how quickly or slowly a dot of
light might increase. As he grew closer, several things
came into view. A wide desk of soft, worn wood made
softer by the glow of a candle. An elderly man at the
desk, head down, writing with a quill in his right hand
that dashed back and forth, quickly at times, and held
still at other times as he looked to his left at a hourglass
while waiting to write more.

The man was writing in a thick book, pages
yellowish that made wrinkly noises when turned.

Directly before the thick book was a candle in a primitive holder formed from a black metal and appeared to have lasted uncountable years of service. Blobs of wax had clumped at the bottom and spilled onto the desk, enough wax that it would take work to lift the candle from the desk.

As the boy approached the desk, he could better see a very old man of more years than he could imagine. His eyebrows were like both black and white spiders, white in their own color but black shadows crawling on the man's head from the dancing candlelight. He had little hair on his head, much on his face, and pinkish, puffy skin, which was barely all the boy could see peering over the edge of the desk. The boy thought the man looked a little like many depictions of Santa Claus, which reminded him of Christmas morning. But as he focused, he could see this was not a happy man. This man had sweat glistening as it ran through wrinkles on his head and face. He seemed out of breath at almost all times, for however much time he imagined he might have been watching.

The boy watched the man and waited to be noticed. He couldn't be sure how long he waited, but for a boy lost in almost complete darkness, anything is too long, especially when looking over the edge of a desk at an unfamiliar, unhappy old man. The boy opened his mouth, closed, opened again, and almost spoke, but each time his eyes became misty and his throat ready to burn. After however much time, he instead reached a hand up so he could put his fingers over the top, like someone trying to peek over a wall that was too high at the zoo to see into the lion cage.

What stopped the boy was not that he was afraid of the man. What stopped him was that he could not see his own fingers when he reached his hands up to the desk. He knew, no question, his hands were up. He could even feel the soft, imperfect wood of the desk. He stepped back and looked down at himself, but he saw nothing. He patted himself, his belly, each arm, and his face. He felt them all but with hands and a body he could not see. That was far more frightening than the the darkness or the man at the desk. The boy had a horribly scary thought.

"No," the man barked. The boy glanced up, confused but focused. "No, I cannot help you."

"I did not ask for help," said the boy.

"You were going to ask. I cannot help you."

"I don't know if I was going to ask for help."

"You were," said the man, his voice slightly softer.

"I don't think that I was going to ask that," the boy said, but he immediately regretted it when the man's face turned from pink to red and the sweat increased along with his breathing.

"No, you are not sorry," the man growled.

"I am not sorry," said the boy, "but I was still going to say it."

"Why?" asked the man. "Why would you say you were sorry if you were not sorry?"

The boy attempted to fix his dry mouth. "Because it is polite."

The quill paused as the man gazed at the hourglass. "Polite will not help you. Only truth will help you here."

"But I don't know where I am."

The quill began again, with the sweating and the hourglass. The boy noticed that the hourglass stopped when the quill stopped.

"If you do not know where you are," said the man, "then you should not be here."

"Maybe I should be here, but I just don't know it," said the boy. "I am sorry if I am asking a lot of questions, but I don't know what else to say."

"Yes you do."

"I don't want to."

"It doesn't matter what you want. Only the truth matters. Ask your question."

The boy looked down again at the self he could not see.

"Am I dead?"

The quill paused only a second before starting again.

"Why do you think that you are dead?"

"Because nothing else would make sense."

"Death makes sense?"

"I don't know."

"If you were dead, you would know if death does or does not make sense. You are not dead."

"Then why am I here?" the boy asked, his voice closer to a whimper.

"Where do you think you are?"

"I think I am where people go when they die."

"What makes you think that?" The man's quill moved more quickly than before.

"Because I cannot see myself. And I have never been anywhere like this."

"You cannot see yourself?" the man asked. "Can you see me?"

"Yes."

"What do you see?"

"I see an old man with a gray beard. Sweating and writing in a book. And a candle."

"The book and candle are not me. What if I said that I am not what you have described?"

"You are not an old man with a gray beard?" the boy asked.

"I did not say if I was or wasn't. I asked, 'What if I am not?' What if I am different than what you see?"

"Why would you be different than what I see?"

"Why would you not see yourself at all?" the man asked as the boys eyes fell to the floor. "If you cannot see yourself as you are, perhaps you cannot see me as I am."

"What do you see when you look at me?"

The man focused on the book and quill as if the boy had not spoken.

"What do I look like?" the boy asked.

"A boy who asks many questions."

The boy sought, or tried to see himself again but still saw nothing. The man continued to push the quill back and forth, occasionally checking the hourglass as the candle flickered and drops of melted wax flowed down the sides until cooling and solidifying.

"You should go," the man said.

"Go where?"

"Where you came from."

"I don't know how to get there," the boy said.

"Go back the way you arrived."

After the boy looked in all directions, "I'm not sure which way I came from."

"Whichever way feels right is where you should go," the man said.

"Can I come back tomorrow?"

"You can do as you choose."

"Do you want me to come back tomorrow?"

"I want you to do what you are supposed to do."

"But I don't know what I'm supposed to do."

"Then you had better learn."

After glancing around, the boy pointed directly away from the front of the desk and said, "I think I should go that way."

"Then go."

"Are you sure I can't stay here with you?"

The man scribbled, paused, and said, "Why would you want to stay with me?"

"Because I'm afraid."

"And when you are here with me, you are not afraid?"

The boy thought before saying, "I don't know what's out there."

"You won't know until you go."

"I guess I will go then," said the boy.

The man pushed the quill, scratching across the yellowed paper while watching both the hourglass and candle. The boy stepped backwards as if a baby had just fallen asleep, then turned and walked away.

———————————

When it seemed like the next day, the boy turned and walked back towards the light, the desk, and the old man. Again the old man said nothing until the boy could no longer stand the silence.

"I think it is the next day, so I came back."

The man said nothing but continued as on the previous day. The boy watched the man's eyes and thought he saw a fraction of a glance his way.

"What are you writing?" the boy asked.

The man took an extra deep breath before continuing to write.

"Can you tell me what you are writing?"

The man continued to write.

"Would you please tell me what you are writing?"

The man continued to write.

"Why won't you tell me what you are writing?"

"Because you would not like the answer."

"Thank you for answering," said the boy. "It is scary to be ignored when you know for sure that someone can hear you. How do you know I wouldn't like the answer?"

"To tell you that would tell you too much," the man said, eyes never leaving the paper or hourglass.

"I don't understand."

"You will have to trust that I know that it is better for you not to know."

"What if you are wrong?"

The man continued to write for longer than the boy preferred.

"What if you are wrong?" the boy repeated.

"If you throw a rock at a dog, what might happen?" the man asked.

"I might hit the dog, but I might not."

"If you don't throw a rock at a dog, what won't happen?"

"I won't hit the dog."

The boy waited for the man to ask something else, but he continued to write and glance at the hourglass. The boy watched carefully for what may have been minutes.

"What is in the hourglass?" the boy asked.

"Sand."

"Why do you have to look at the hourglass before you write?"

"That is too difficult to explain."

"You look at the hourglass before you write. Is that true?"

The man did not answer for what may have been minutes.

"So," the boy said, "it is yes. You see something in the hourglass before you write. I guess it tells you what to write."

"It does not."

"If it does not tell you what to write, then it shows you what to write."

The boy waited, but the man said nothing.

"There is something you look at in the hourglass, and then you know what to write. Is that true?" He watched as the man continued to write and be silent.

"There are things written on the grains of sand, and you are writing what you see."

"That is not correct," said the man as the tail of the quill danced more sharply and his sweating increased.

"You cannot lie, can you?" the boy said.

The man stayed silent.

"If I am wrong, you tell me so. But if I am right, you sometimes stay silent because you don't want me to know the truth."

The man stayed silent. The boy said many things to himself.

"Are you writing the names of dead people?"

"Why would you ask me that question?"

"Because I think this place has something to do with death."

"Why do you think this place has something to do with death?"

"I told you yesterday, because it is like nothing I have ever seen."

"Have you ever seen an octopus in the ocean?"

"No," said the boy.

"If you saw an octopus in the ocean, would you think it was death because it is nothing like you have ever seen?"

"No, but you are just trying to confuse me by avoiding my question." The boy studied the man's face. "Yesterday I asked what you see when you look at me, but you did not answer. I am a ten-year old boy. Do you see a boy when you look at me?"

The man silently wrote.

"Can you see me at all?"

"Yes."

"Why won't you tell me what you see?"

"Because you would not like what I would say."

"Sometimes we must know things, even when we don't like them." After saying that, the boy tilted his head down to again try to see himself. Still seeing nothing, he tried again to feel his own being, and again he could, however, something was different. He concentrated more with his fingertips and realized that his arms, hands, and chest were not those of a 10-year old boy. His jaw and hair were not those of a 10-year old boy either.

"How old am I?" he asked of the man with the quill.

"How old do you think you are?"

"Am I less than twelve?"

No answer.

"Less than twenty?"

No answer.

"Less than thirty?"

No answer.

"Less than fifty?"

"Ten is less than fifty."

The boy paused. "So I am somewhere between forty and fifty, but I feel like I am ten. Why do I feel like I am ten?"

"That is a question for yourself," said the old man as he scribbled in the book.

"I can't see myself, but you can see me, so you would know."

"I never said I could see you."

"You never answered the question, which means that you can. So, why won't you tell me?"

"I never said I wouldn't tell you."

"But you won't tell me, which means you can but you choose not to. Perhaps you believe I would not benefit from knowing. It would help me figure out something that you do not want me to figure out." The boy thought more carefully, turning slightly away from the desk. "If I am really older, then I must be dead."

"I said you are not dead."

"And you can't lie. So I must be dying."

"I never said you were dying." The old man scribbled further.

"Does this place have to do with death or those who are dying?"

The man stayed silent as the boy watched and waited until what seemed long enough.

"So, I am dying. That much is true. Please, tell me why I am dying. Tell me if I can still be saved or is it just a matter of time."

"It is just a matter of time," the old man said, "but that is true for everyone who is alive, not just you."

"But for me to be here now means that my death must be coming soon."

"That does not have to be true," said the old man.

"My death might not be soon," said the boy, "but my life must be at risk right this moment wherever I might really be." He tried to read the old man's eyes. "Do you know where my body is right now?"

"I do not."

"Do you know anything about my body right now?"

"I do not."

"Do you agree that my body is in the process of dying right now?"

The old man continued to write before saying, "It is possible."

The boy's face fell. "Is there anything I can do to save myself?"

"It is possible," the old man said softly.

"Can you tell me what I can do?"

The man continued to write.

"Then you can tell me, but you prefer not to tell me."

The man continued to write.

"You have nothing to say?" asked the boy. He slapped the front of the desk. The old man did not flinch, but the boy turned away for a moment and walked in a small circle. When he came back to the desk, his eyes were slightly higher than before. He could see more of the surface of the desk and was more focused on the moment.

"I am somewhere dying. You can help save me but refuse. True or false?"

The man continued to write silently.

"Do you not care about life so that you would just let mine go?" the boy said with force as the old man kept writing. "You are going to just let me die instead of telling me what I could do to help myself live?"

The man glanced up at the hourglass, then put his head down to write despite the sweat in his eyes.

"No heart? No respect for life? No desire to do good? Is that what you are?" the boy demanded. He put his hands over his face, bent his knees down to a crouch, and then stood up again. When he did, he was again slightly taller and able to fully see the desk much like any other desk he had ever stood before. He no longer imagined himself as a 10-year old boy. Although still unable to see himself, something within his own presence was becoming a grown man.

"Is this how you treat people?" His voice deepened. "Does it make any difference to you if people live or die? You won't lift a finger to help someone who is dying? Do you get some kind of fun out of death? You get paid something extra for each death that comes through your little hourglass over there? Is there some kind of bonus at the end of the month for how many deaths you can write down?"

The quill paused for a very short time as the old man looked up at the younger man. "I will say no more. You will ask no more. You will make your own choices and bother me no more." Then he put his head down and continued to write.

"Great," barked the younger man. "You seem to have some kind of power here, but you would rather just keep writing with your fancy pen. So I will go do something helpful for this world! I will figure out for myself where I am and what I am supposed to be doing. I don't need your help to save myself because all you can do is whatever you are told to do! You are nothing more than a slave to that desk and pen and book and hourglass. I at least have the strength and desire to make a difference to someone!"

The boy, who was now a man, turned from the desk and sprinted away. Even without the darkness, he still would not have been able to see clearly with tear-filled eyes, streaming like the sweat he had seen on the old man's head and face. As he ran, he no longer felt as small as before, but even internally realized that he was older and taller.

After as many minutes as he could not count, his legs grew weary. He slowed and turned slightly, unable to see the point of light that he had been running from but then found a new point of light up ahead. With renewed vigor, his legs churned forward as this new point of light slowly grew.

The point became a circle, and the circle became a room. The room became a familiar basement, dark and with a desk on which was a chair, piece of paper, pen, and pocket watch. He saw himself sitting at the desk and writing. He walked behind himself and read what he was writing.

Dear Ann,

*I am sorry for all that has gone
wrong. I really tried my best, but I
have become nothing more than an
embarrassment to all of us. Please
find a way to let the children know
how much I love them and how
sorry I am that they did not have a
better father. Please give this watch
to our son. It was given to me by my
father. I don't deserve this watch,
nor you, nor our son, nor your love.*

*Love,
John*

The man watched himself put down the pen, stand,
and walk towards a chair in the middle of the basement.
He accidentally knocked over an empty wine bottle on
the floor and stepped up on the chair. A loop of rope
hung from a ceiling beam, and the man watched himself
fix the rope around his neck and then kick over the chair.

The man struggled with himself, attempting to hold
his legs up and slacken the noose. He screamed for help,
but panic and fear sapped his strength quickly. His cries
fell unheard as he tried again to lift himself higher. He
screamed and cursed at himself to fight and lift his arms
to remove the noose, but he could not hear himself.

———————————

A man walked down a dark hallway towards a dot of
light that looked far enough way that it might take an

hour for him to reach it. He was very surprised as it grew far more quickly than he expected, although he wasn't really sure just how quickly or slowly a dot of light might increase. As he grew closer, several things came into view. A wide desk of soft, worn wood made softer by the glow of a candle. An elderly man at the desk, head down, writing with a quill in his right hand that dashed back and forth, quickly at times, and held still at other times as he looked to his left at a hourglass while waiting to write more.

The man was writing in a thick book, pages yellowish that made wrinkly noises when turned. Directly before the thick book was a candle in a primitive holder formed from a black metal and appeared to have lasted uncountable years of service. Blobs of wax had clumped at the bottom and spilled onto the desk, enough wax that it would take work to lift the candle from the desk.

As the young man approached the desk, he could see two distant doorways behind each of the old man's weary shoulders. The old man looked down at him, back at the book, and scribbled something. Then, while writing again in the book, he pointed to the left doorway.

"Do I get to choose?" the young man asked.

The old man looked up from the book and said, "You already did."

2. The Wish

One day, while I was driving to pick up my daughter, I thought about wishes and wishing fountains. Originally, I thought about putting a wishing fountain in front of my house just to make some easy money. Then I thought about what might happen when people toss coins into a fountain and make a wish. What if there were a group of people assigned to review each wish and vote on whether or not to grant it?

Mrs. O'Reilly lifted her aching elbows above the table before dropping the five-inch thick binder with a thump before leaning on the solid mahogany table until catching her breath. As she took a seat at the far left of the table, Mr. O'Reilly let go of his walker and landed in his seat at the far right. One by one, other council members reached their seats by walker, cane, or with the help of an aide until all five had taken their places at what was shaped like a giant letter C.

Mr. Fuhr tapped his microphone, instead of speaking into it, several times until he was certain it was working. The final chair, inside the C-shaped table, was filled when Miss McGowan plugged her stenotype machine into a white extension cord. Once she was satisfied, she nodded to Chairman Bonowitz, which prompted him to tap his gavel and call that week's meeting to order.

"Mrs. O'Reilly," Chairman Bonowitz said, "how many requests since last week?" She found the right page while tilting her head enough for her bifocals to do their job. The committee waited.

"Dammit, Margaret," grumbled Mr. Rizzo, "every meeting starts on the same page. How can you not be ready, after all these years?"

"Now, now, Jerry," Mr. O'Reilly interrupted, "it's not the same page every time."

"It's not the SAME page, but it's always the second page in the binder," said Mr. Rizzo. "I was secretary last year, so I know what I'm talking about. You're just defending your wife."

"Ex-wife, I'll remind you," said Mr. O'Reilly while raising a finger and nodding.

"Then why doesn't she change her name?" asked Mr. Rizzo.

"None of your business," said Mr. O'Reilly.

"Calm down, both of you," said Mrs. O'Reilly. "Mr. Chairman, we have three-hundred forty-seven requests since last week."

"You shitting me?" said Mr. Rizzo.

"I know," said Mr. O'Reilly. "That's got to be another record."

"What the Hell is going on?" yelled Mr. Rizzo.

"Hey," said Mr. O'Reilly, "things are tough up there. Economy, depression, divorce."

Chairman Bonowitz tapped his gavel three times. "Excuse me, folks, but Miss McGowan has a question. Yes, Miss McGowan."

She looked at the paper tape exiting the top of the machine. "Is 'Hell' capitalized?"

"Aw, who cares," griped Mr. Rizzo. "It's not like we won't know what the Hell you're talking about either way. Just type whatever the Hell you want."

Chairman Bonowitz tapped his gavel twice. "Mr. Rizzo, maybe if you said 'Hell' less often, she would be able to type faster."

Mrs. O'Reilly pulled her microphone closer. "My mother always said that people only curse if they don't have a strong enough vocabulary."

There was an unplanned moment of silence while Mr. Rizzo smiled more proudly than he deserved. The others rolled their eyes and checked their copies of the agenda.

Chairman Bonowitz tapped his gavel, this time a little harder.

"Mr. Rizzo," he called, "can we get a treasury report?"

The round, gray man put down his cell phone, found a sheet of paper, and stood. "A little under a grand." Mr. Rizzo began to sit until the gavel tapped again, stopping him in mid-sit before he stood again, palms open. "What?"

"Mr. Rizzo," said Mrs. O'Reilly, "you know fully well we need itemization."

The grumpy man scratched himself where he shouldn't when with others, looked at the paper again, and cleared his throat. "There was $844 in quarters, $32.90 in dimes, $55.45 in nickels, and $13.27 in pennies. Total was $945.62."

"Thank you, Mr. Treasurer," said Mrs. O'Reilly, "but I would like a detailed average on that, please."

"Son of a-," Mr. Rizzo began, then shuffled a few more papers. "There were 5,082 requests and $945.62 at an average of 18.6 cents per request. Slightly higher than last month but pretty much on par for the year."

"Thank you, Mr. Treasurer," said Mrs. O'Reilly, smiling slightly more than before. However, before anyone could get comfortable again, Mr. Rizzo quickly fired into his microphone.

"You want me to believe those details really make a difference? It wasn't good enough just to say it was a little under a grand?" said the angry Italian. "What's your problem?" Chairman Bonowitz raised his gavel. "Bang that friggin' thing again and I'll jam up your - "

Before Mr. Rizzo could label exactly where he would jam the gavel, Chairman Bonowitz yelled, "Yes, Miss McGowan?"

"I'm sorry to interrupt again, but I have to ask if I'm supposed to put a G on the end of friggin'."

"I-I don't understand," said the chairman.

"When he says 'frigging,' he's not really pronouncing the G at the end," the young woman said between text messages, "so I'm not sure if I should put the G or not. I mean, it belongs there, but maybe I should leave the G off because he doesn't pronounce it."

"Hey, Sweetie," said Mr. Rizzo with a smile that might cause children to cry, "you type whateeeever makes you happy."

There was another unintentional moment of silence as everyone, except Mr. Fuhr, was in quiet awe as Mr. Fuhr slowly rose to his feet. Even Mr. Rizzo paused from scratching himself just to watch Mr. Fuhr, upright, and raising a finger to get the attention of Chairman Bonowitz.

"The, um, chair recognizes Mr. Fuhr," said the man with the gavel at rest. All eyes were on Mr. Fuhr. Mrs. O'Reilly thought about what his voice sounded like, but it didn't take her long to remember it fondly. Miss McGowan was quite certain she had never typed his name in any council minutes that she had ever recorded in the past quarter. There was no question from anyone, not even Mr. Rizzo, that if Mr. Fuhr was finally about to speak, it must be something serious.

"I." Cleared his throat. "I was." Focused tightly on the agenda. "I was looking at some of the items requested this week." Adjusted his glasses. "And one." Cleared his throat again. "And one was particularly interesting." Mr. Fuhr sat down again.

Several members at the table, especially Mr. and Mrs. O'Reilly, glanced towards each other and then back to Mr. Fuhr. Everyone waited, especially the fingers of Miss McGowan.

"And?" asked Chairman Bonowitz.

Mr. Fuhr stood again. "I'm sorry. What?"

"You said one item was particularly interesting."

"Yes?"

"Which one? What was so interesting?" asked Mrs. O'Reilly.

"Oh." Mr. Fuhr's skin was nearly as white as his starched, short-sleeve shirt and as far from his black tie as humanly possible. He held the agenda closer to his face while again adjusting his glasses. "This boy. Who made a wish."

"A request," said Chairman Bonowitz.

Mr. Rizzo exhaled before standing and after gaining a nod from the chairman. "Mr. Fuhr, with all due respect, lots of kids make lots of," air quotes, "requests every week. As you know, we grant about half of them. That's why we sit here like idiots every week and listen to gavel boy over here pounding on the table." Mrs. O'Reilly's mouth dropped. "But, please tell us what's so special about this one that was soooo special you need to break procedure."

"Well," Mr. Fuhr tilted the page to avoid a glare from the brilliant lights above the table, "he submitted his request on 33rd street."

"So?" asked Mr. Rizzo.

"He lives on 68th street."

"So?"

Mr. Fuhr's hands began to shake. "W-well. If he submitted his request that far from home, shouldn't we find out why? It's probably important."

"Yes, well," began Chairman Bonowitz, "anything else?"

"Sure, sure. He submitted his request at 1:09 pm on Monday."

"So?" asked Mr. Rizzo.

"So he should have been in school," said Mr. Fuhr.

"So that gives us more of a reason to reject it," said Mrs. O'Reilly.

"Why?"

"Because he should have been in school. Not cutting class," said Mrs. O'Reilly.

"But that's my point," said Mr. Fuhr. "If a kid cuts class, they do something fun. Why would he take the time to submit a request? Any other kid would have used that money for a soda or downloading a song from iTunes. Not a request."

"How much did he invest?" asked Chairman Bonowitz.

"Two dollars," said Mr. Fuhr.

"Two bucks?" shouted Mr. Rizzo. "You sure?"

"You're the treasurer," pointed Chairman Bonowitz. "You should know."

"I just thought it was a typo," said Mr. Rizzo.

"I don't make typos," snapped Miss McGowan.

"Nobody spends two bucks on a request. I thought it was twenty cents."

"You thought wrong, Mr. Rizzo," said Mr. Fuhr.

"Hey," the Italian grew louder, "you don't speak for a year, and now you're telling me what I'm doing wrong?"

"Mr. Rizzo," said Mr. Fuhr, "it doesn't matter *who* tells you that you did wrong. What matter is *what* you did wrong."

"Wrongly," interrupted Mrs. O'Reilly.

"Jeez, will you stop?" begged Mr. Rizzo.

"I'm just saying," said Mrs. O'Reilly.

"And I'm just saying to shut up or I just might - "

The chairman slammed the gavel on the C-shaped table, preventing Mr. Rizzo from threatening bodily harm upon the wife of last year's chairman.

"Do you mind if we take a break?" Chairman Bonowitz said to Miss McGowan.

"Already?" she said. "I guess so. I have to pee anyway."

The gavel struck once more, then rested, and everyone removed themselves from their chairs for ten minutes.

Miss McGowan returned to her chair, rendering Mr. Rizzo unable to stare at the roundness of her skirt. Chairman Bonowitz, similarly unable, hit the gavel.

"Now, where were we?" he asked as Mr. Fuhr stood.

"We were talking about the boy with the two-dollar request."

"Does the boy have a name?" asked Mrs. O'Reilly.

"Vincent," said Mr. Fuhr.

"I approve," laughed Mr. Rizzo who then laughed even more after catching a snarl from Mrs. O'Reilly. The loud Italian glanced around for approval but found none, or at least none that anyone would publically admit.

"Age?" asked Chairman Bonowitz.

"He's 13," said Mr. Fuhr.

"What does the kid want?" asked Mr. Rizzo.

"He said," Mr. Fuhr flipped another page in the agenda, "he would like - "

"Whoa, hold on," whined Mr. O'Reilly. "Why aren't we going in order? Procedures for this committee have been set for more than a hundred years. Probably two hundred. If we change procedure, there needs to be an explanation, a motion, a second, and a vote."

"Hey," said Mr. Rizzo, "does it really matter what request we review first? Who the Hell cares? We read them all eventually anyway. Right?"

"Oh, sure," said Mrs. O'Reilly. She patted the back of her bluish hair but knew that not one hair could have possibly been out of place. "Let's just throw out the rules and do whatever we want."

"I'm good with that," said Mr. Rizzo.

"I was being facetious," said Mrs. O'Reilly.

"Seriously," said Mr. Rizzo, "what's the difference? This kid first, this kid last, tenth, two-hundred and eleventh. Who cares?"

Chairman Bonowitz hit the gavel again. "Please, please, with the bickering. How about the two of you just shut up and get married?"

Mr. Fuhr stood again, raising a shaky finger until Chairman Bonowitz nodded his way.

"I-I'm very sorry that I broke procedure, but considering where this boy appeared on the list, it probably wouldn't be hours before we got to him. I just thought this one was an emergency or something, and we should get to him first."

Chairman Bonowitz clicked his pen. "Is there a motion to move, uh, Vincent first?"

"Motion," said Mr. Fuhr.

"Second?"

"Second," barked Mr. Rizzo.

"Anyone against?" asked Chairman Bonowitz.

Mrs. O'Reilly raised a hand while glaring at Mr. O'Reilly, who was not raising a hand.

"Motion carries," said the Chairman, one tap on the gavel. "Mr. Fuhr, please read the file on Vincent."

"Vincent Willet, born January 30, age 13. No siblings, lives with his mother in a one-bedroom apartment on 68th street."

"There's a good bakery there," said Mrs. O'Reilly, drawing a nod from Miss McGowan, who never broke stride while typing.

"Goes to PS 39, average student, played Little League for three years but plans to skip this year. No explanation given, but I have a guess. Nobody in his family has ever attended any of his games, and I think he feels a little ignored."

"You said he lives with his mother?" asked the chairman. "Is there a father?"

"I quote from his request," Mr. Fuhr flipped a page. "I wish I knew who my father is."

The group sat in silence. The only sound was Miss McGowan's fingers catching up to what was last said, then she waited.

Mr. O'Reilly scratched at his sparse, gray hair. "I sure miss those days of kids requesting an A on a test or a bike for Christmas."

"Christmas is not our jurisdiction," said the chairman.

"I'm just saying."

The chairman nodded and smiled. "I know," he said softly, then loudly, "Initial vote for Vincent to know who his father is. Mrs. O'Reilly, read the role."

"Mr. Rizzo?"

"Yes," said Mr. Rizzo.

"Mr. Fuhr?"

"Yes."

"Mr. O'Reilly?"

"No."

"And a 'no' from me," said Mrs. O'Reilly.

"Two for yes and two for no," said the chairman before hitting the gavel. "Rules are for the chairman to break the tie, but I will need more information before I can vote. Questions? Statements?"

"Yes," said the woman who voted 'no,' "he's done just fine with his mother all these years. Why mess things up? Why confuse him by bringing his father into his life now? His father is probably some kind of - "

"Hey," interrupted Mr. Rizzo, "hey, Mrs. Manhater. A kid has a right to know his father."

"If his father wanted to know him," said Mr. O'Reilly, "he would know him. The father has some rights here too. Maybe he has a reason."

"Maybe he doesn't even know he's the father," said Mr. Fuhr.

"Maybe he's better off not knowing he's the father," said Mrs. O'Reilly.

"Rule 13-point-4, subsection B," said the chairman, "no wish shall be granted if there is the potential for great negative impact on someone else either involved or uninvolved."

"But there's also potential for *positive* impact," said Mr. Rizzo.

"Maybe positive for him," said Mr. O'Reilly, "but maybe negative for his father."

"But he isn't asking to *meet* his father," said Mr. Fuhr. "Read his request yourself. He just wants to *know* who his father is."

Mrs. O'Reilly parked her fists on her hips. "You know once he has the man's name, the boy will try to find him."

"We don't need to care about that," said Mr. Rizzo. "Those are the risks that anyone takes anytime they wish for anything. How many times have people said, 'Be careful what you wish for'? They don't say it for nothing."

"The boy made a wish," said Chairman Bonowitz. "He's got a right to make a wish for his betterment. Repercussions and consequences are always inherent in any given action. It's the chance you take."

"He's only thirteen," said Mrs. O'Reilly. "This is rather powerful."

"Not to mention the effect it might have on both his mother *and* his father," added Mr. O'Reilly.

"What about the effect of never knowing his father?" said Mr. Rizzo.

As before, they listened while Miss McGowan's keys clicked until she caught up. Then the five-member committee stared back and forth, each pair of "yes" and "no" voters waiting for Chairman Bonowitz to cast a deciding vote.

"Are there any volunteers for a research sub-committee?" the chairman asked. "We would need two."

"Me," said Mr. Fuhr.

"Me too," said Mr. Rizzo.

"Rules are that sub-committees must be two people, one from each side of the vote," said Mrs. O'Reilly. "I volunteer to join Mr. Fuhr."

"Any objections?" When nobody spoke after a handful of seconds, the gavel struck. "Mr. Fuhr and Mrs. O'Reilly are now the subcommittee in the request submitted by Vincent," he glanced at the paper, "Vincent Willet. Take a copy of the relevant pages from the agenda and be prepared to leave before the end of the day."

"What about the rest of the agenda?" asked Mr. O'Reilly.

The gavel smacked once more, more loudly than any other in the session.

"After lunch," said Bonowitz, already out of his chair.

"But it's not even eleven o'clock yet," argued Mr. O'Reilly.

"Eddie," said Mr. Bonowitz, "you were chairman last year. My turn now."

Before reaching the top step on the way out of the 64th Street station, Mrs. O'Reilly and Mr. Fuhr were already squinting against the late afternoon sun. Seeing Mr. Fuhr's difficulty, Mrs. O'Reilly offered, "The handrail, Al. Use the handrail. Pull yourself up." He watched as she seemed to be winning a game of "tug of war" but pulling a metal bar instead of a rope.

"Thanks," Mr. Fuhr said. "I can't even remember the last time I was up here. So bright."

"I think it's fall. The sun is setting earlier this time of year."

"Leaves are mostly green with a little bit of yellow, I'd say it's the last week of September. Gosh, that was my favorite time of year. Beginning of football season and pennant races winding up. World Series starts soon. I wonder if the Mets have won yet." He glanced left and right to find Mrs. O'Reilly. "Which way?"

"This way," she pointed. "Come on."

He followed, but it only took a few minutes before he was out of breath.

"Can they see us?" Mr. Fuhr asked.

"Not usually. You should know this."

"I don't remember."

"When was the last time you were on a subcommittee?"

"I don't remember."

"Al," she shook her head, "you need to get out more."

After another half block, he said, "Thank you."

"For what?" She pulled the front of her three-quarter sleeve sweater more closed in front of her, then buttoned it.

"You called me Al. That's nice." He tried to keep pace, but she occasionally had to slow down for him.

"Did you think I forgot?" He didn't answer immediately. "Do you remember my name?"

"Margie."

"Margaret," she corrected.

"Sorry." He kept pace slightly better. "It used to be Margie."

"A lot of things 'used to be,' but I'm glad you remember." Although he could not see from behind her, she had a smile bigger than any other going back a month. So did he.

Mrs. O'Reilly flipped one page and another of a packet stapled at the upper-left corner.

"Third floor," she said. "That one, with the open windows."

They craned their necks to look over the heads of pedestrians on the sidewalk, but they could only stretch a short time before their combined two-hundred plus years of age forced them to look down for a spell before gazing up again.

"That one with the plants?" Mr. Fuhr asked.

"I think so."

He looked down again and noticed how the pedestrians were veering left and right around them.

"I thought you said these people can't see us," he said.

"They can't see us, but they can sense us."

"They just know?"

"Something like that," she said. "Their instincts just tell them to move around us. It's got something to do with life forces. I really can't explain it. Sorry."

"What if they didn't move?"

"I don't know. I haven't been up here for about four years."

"But you knew exactly where to go? You knew there was a great bakery up on this street?"

She opened her mouth, shut it, then opened it again. "I come up here sometimes, but not on official business."

"Then why?"

She glanced away, squinting at the sun reflecting off a brick apartment building before them. "My daughter."

"YOUR daughter?"

"MY daughter."

"As long as you're sure about that." He turned stiffly and only then noticed the deli behind them. He stepped carefully to the door and drew a handful of attention when he pulled it open. He drew no additional attention when he entered unseen.

"What are you doing?" Mrs. O'Reilly hushed.

"I want a corned beef sandwich."

"You can't have a sandwich. And it's called a Reuben."

"It's called a Reuben if it's grilled with Swiss cheese, sauerkraut, Thousand Island dressing, and served with cole slaw and a pickle."

"Can we just get across the street and see what's going on with the boy and his mother?"

"You don't have to be so bossy about it," Mr. Fuhr said.

"Apparently I do because you won't follow procedures."

"Same ol' Margie. Thinks she knows more than everyone else."

She exited the deli but stopped on the sidewalk as pedestrians flowed around here.

"Let me tell you something," she pointed. "There are two of us here. One of us knows more than the other, and that's a fact. I've done this more often and more recently than you, and that's a fact. So who do you think probably knows more than the other? Me or you?"

Instead of waiting for an answer, she barged through traffic while he followed as quickly as he could. Some cars slowed as drivers either believed the light was about to change or got hit with glare from the setting sun. Others thought for sure they saw a squirrel or something make a quick dash for the other side.

The slow pair reached the third floor apartment on the agenda and waited only a few seconds before a girl emerged from the next apartment and knocked where Mrs. O'Reilly and Mr. Fuhr stood. A shadow passed on the other side of the door's peep hole before the door opened to reveal a happy boy.

Mrs. O'Reilly folded her papers and said, "That's him."

"Hi," Vincent said to the girl.

"Hey." They smiled at each other, she a few inches taller despite being a year younger. "You got homework?"

"Finished it," he said.

"I'm having trouble with math." She tilted her head as if hearing something behind her. His eyes shifted a little, as if a glint of light had come from down the hall. "You watching TV?"

"Reading."

"What book?"

"Third Narnia book. *Voyage of the Dawn Treader.*"

"Who's your favorite character so far?"

"Reepicheep, of course."

They paused, neither knowing why nor that two people slid past them and into the boy's apartment. Vincent snapped his head specifically to move his dark hair out of his blue eyes, specifically to get a better look at her dark hair and blue eyes, then invited her in.

"You sure your mom won't mind?" she asked.

"No, but come on in."

He closed the door, locked it, and followed as she moved to the sofa. Most afternoons they knelt on the cushions, folded their arms on the backrest, and gazed at the city street to simply watch people walk by.

"What's her name?" Mr. Fuhr asked Mrs. O'Reilly.

"Pretty sure this is Abbey." She flipped through the six pages of the investigation packet. "Lives next door. They spend most afternoons together until their mothers get home."

"Think she's important?" he asked.

"Come with me." Mrs. O'Reilly stepped through the open window next to the sofa and walked along the ledge until she was standing, then sitting sideways, legs dangling, facing the two kids. Mr. Fuhr followed less confidently than his partner.

"You big baby," she barked. "Even if you fell, nothing would happen."

"It's still a little scary."

"Sit," the old woman said. "Look at them." From their vantage point, they could see both faces, dark complexions, narrow noses, and dimpled foreheads. Mrs. O'Reilly turned, perched still on the ledge, and scanned the people below. She focused on as many as possible until finally a girl about the children's age stopped.

"Hey, Abbey!" The two girls waved at each other, and then Mrs. O'Reilly turned to Mr. Fuhr.

"There. You happy? Her name - "

"I heard. Abbey!" he snapped.

"What?" Abbey said, leaning towards Vincent.

"I didn't say anything," Vincent said.

"Nice going, big mouth," said Mrs. O'Reilly.

"You called my name," said Abbey.

"Sorry," said Mr. Fuhr.

"No I didn't," said Vincent.

"I heard my name," said Abbey.

"Wasn't me," the boy said, eyebrows arched. "You sure?"

"I don't know," Abbey said. "Maybe my hearing is going."

"That would be really weird," said Vincent, "because that's what my mother says about me."

"Maybe you just don't listen." She kicked a throw pillow at him.

"Or maybe you're just a stupid girl." He gently sent it back.

They shared an uneasy silence before staring out the window again, waiting and hoping for something interesting to happen. Abbey broke the silence.

"Your mom still trying to move?"

"I guess so."

"You still think it's because of my mom?" Abbey asked.

"I know they still don't like each other, but I don't think that's why she wants to move. I heard her on the phone talking about a homeless guy who keeps following her. Guy was even calling her name, and it was freaking her out," Vincent said.

"I think I've seen that guy. I told my mom to give him a dollar, and she looked like she was about to cry. But that's not a reason to move. I don't want you to move." She tried to change the subject. "What's for dinner? Pizza?"

"No way. You would eat that every day if you could."

"Yeah, I would," she stressed.

"I'm making chicken Parmesan."

"Can you teach me how to make that? My mom gets home so late, it would be cool if I can learn to cook. Maybe it'll cheer her up a little. Nothing else seems to help."

"Yeah," said Vincent, "I know what you mean. Sometimes I'm convinced that neither of them like either of us very much."

"I don't know about my mom not liking you," Abbey said, "but there's no doubt your mom hates me."

"But I could probably say the same thing."

"See?" said Mr. Fuhr to Mrs. O'Reilly. "The boy needs to know his father. They both do. His mother hates him, he's got a girl for a best friend, and he's teaching her how to cook."

"What's wrong with that?" asked Mrs. O'Reilly.

"He should be out playing football or baseball. Not teaching her how to cook. Maybe she should be teaching him how to cook."

"Can I help?" Abbey asked.

"You can start by washing your hands," said Vincent.

They left the couch. Vincent headed for the kitchen as Abbey clicked on the radio that sat on a shelf amidst Vincent's bookshelves, which held more titles than her classroom.

"The stations are all set to my mom's music, so you're going to have to find something we would like," Vincent called from the kitchen as the two elderly folk flowed back into the room from the ledge and watched from the now empty couch.

"You want to ruin these two?" Mrs. O'Reilly asked.

"What are you talking about?" Mr. Fuhr asked.

"Look how nicely they get along. They need each other. What do you think will happen if he finds out who his father is?"

"What's that got to do with them being friends?"

"Son of a," she caught herself. "You don't see it, do you?"

"See what? Holy wow, why do women always think men are mind readers? Just tell us what the heck is going on, and we won't have to guess wrong."

"Come with me," she said as she reached for his hand. Although still not visible, they disappeared and reappeared about thirty blocks away in an alley between a bank and a convenience store across the street from an empty school.

"What are we doing here?" Mr. Fuhr asked as the silent woman walked to the top of a set of stairs that descended below street level and down to the store's basement. They peered over the edge of the railing to see a man's legs protruding from a few sheets of cardboard.

"Who do you think that is?"

"The boy's father?"

"Yes, but there's more."

"Oh boy, here we go again," grumped Mr. Fuhr while pointing a finger. "Can't you just - " He stopped, lowered his finger, and tried to put his unsteady hands in his pockets. She smiled, but wasn't happy, as a wave of awareness swept across his face.

"That man has not seen either of them since each of their first birthdays. Once their mothers found out, he packed up and left in the middle of the night."

"So they are step brother and sister?" Mr. Fuhr asked.

"Half brother and sister."

"I guess that's why Abbey's mother is divorced? Her husband found out?"

"She was single. Ten years younger than Vincent's mother. Didn't even have a boyfriend. Had just graduated college and was trying to get her career started. Sometimes Vincent's mother worked late, and the father would pay a visit next door."

"Oh, that's horrible."

"It's horrible that her career never happened, but it's never horrible that a child was born."

Mrs. O'Reilly turned from the basement stairs and led them from the alley to the sidewalk where leaves were golden, breezes were cool, and jackets were worn but not yet zippered. They continued across the street to the school playground, stopping in front of a merry-go-round. He put a foot on one of the hexagonal benches, each a different color. She wobbled, climbed, then sat at the top where the six sides formed a pyramid. He gave it a push, sending her in a slow circle as a mother with a stroller watched curiously at the merry-go-round that suddenly powered itself. The old couple tried not to laugh as the woman quickly gained distance.

"Hey," he said, "why did it take you eighty years to finally tell me that I wasn't Marie's father?"

"Was it really eighty years?" she asked, voice softening.

"Eighty years."

"Well, I think, maybe," she paused.

"No maybe. There's only one truth. That's all I'm asking for." He reached his foot out and stopped the merry-go-round so that she was facing him."

"I was afraid you would stop talking to me," she said.

"I *did* stop talking to you. Because you wouldn't tell me."

She climbed down and reached for his hand to steady herself. Once she stepped off the merry-go-round, he kept hold of her hand. They walked beneath the October trees as leaves, both on the ground and falling, seemed to glide around them.

"Does your husband know? I mean about me?"

"Yes."

"Does he know he is Marie's father?"

"He knows. But he didn't always know. Just as I didn't tell you, I didn't tell him either. Honestly, I just wasn't sure for a long time."

"Really? We didn't have genetic testing back then, so how did you figure it out?"

As they passed the front of a brick building, she saw a penny, heads up, next to the fountain that commemorated the Columbus Avenue Middle School on 33rd Street. She picked up the penny, flipped it into the fountain, and walked on. He tightened his hold of her hand and pulled her a little closer. Another block later, they faded away like shadows do when the sun ducks behind a cloud.

3. The Sweeper

*One of my favorite debates is about the
creation of the Universe. I have written
thousands of words in blog comments on
Rogerebert.com about it, participating in
many "battles." While sitting in a boring
teacher's workshop, I picked up my pen and
wrote what might have been my first real
short story. It is an alternative for those
who are stuck between Creationism, aka
Intelligent Design, and the Big Bang Theory.
This is my compromise of two theories.*

A short man with an imperfect mustache pushed a
broom across a concrete floor for what seemed like and
may have been the millionth time. He could have
believed he had been pushing the broom since the
beginning of time and would still be pushing when time
was all over, but he never complained, nor would ever
he dream of complaining, nor would he ever dream.
 Above him was a black ceiling that looked more empty
than black except for occasional flashes of light. Some
lights faded just as quickly as they had appeared, gone
before anyone even noticed they had been there. Some
lights had been burning since before the man with the
broom had ever arrived and some would burn long
beyond him. Some had not been there yesterday, and
some would not be there tomorrow.

Surrounding the man were cubes of space lined up in
all directions as far as he could see or had ever walked.
Each cube extended into a hole in the floor and was eight

of the man's steps on all four sides, and he knew this for sure because he had walked past them endlessly, every day, as far back as he could remember. Although the cubes were empty spaces that descended into the floor, these cubes also had short, knee-high walls that extended above the floor. The walls were topped by a wrought-iron railing another foot above the wall, making each of them like an empty animal pen at a zoo. Each railing had a hook holding a clipboard that held seven laminated papers.

The cubes were in grid form. The Boss preferred to call them "projects" instead of cubes because "it makes everything seem more important," he once said to the man with the broom. To the man with the broom, it would have been like standing on a waffle with endless depressions in all directions, but he had never seen a waffle, so he would not know.

The man did nothing more than sweep the floor that surrounded the cubes and, as per specific instructions, he never once reached inside the railings. He would, however, occasionally walk close enough to feel that the air was much colder on the other side of that railing. There was no floor inside each square, just an emptiness, similar to the blackness above. In fact, both the blackness above and in the bottom of the cubes looked exactly the same, as if there were mirrors in the bottom of the cubes that reflected the ceiling.

In each square there were various objects randomly scattered left, right, high, and low. They were mostly spherical objects, some clustered and some isolated and alone. Some were brilliant balls of yellow, orange, or white, and some were as dark as coal, barely or not at all visible against the emptiness of the cube. Some objects were different shades of red and brown. Some slowly turned, traveled around the cube, or both. Some stayed still as others sped by. Some moved so imperceptibly that the man with the broom could not notice a difference unless he passed by again a very long time after. If an object reached the edge of its cube, it immediately dropped to the floor that ran like a path between the countless cubes. Then the man with the broom would sweep them away, which was the sole reason why there even was a man with a broom who happened to have an imperfect mustache.

"Careful with the broom, Eddie," said the Boss.

"Si, Señor."

"Did you sweep Gamma recently?"

"No, Señor."

"We have a T-5 there, and it's falling back to a T-6. I thought maybe you had swept a little too hard."

"No, Señor."

The Boss held a clipboard with the identifier "Duro 1638" at the top of all seven pages. Some pages had line graphs and pie charts that updated themselves when necessary. On the front page was a box that had had "T-4" in it when the Boss had picked it from its hook, but then it showed "T-5" when he put it back.

"We are losing this one too," he grumbled through a tight jaw. He exhaled and huffed. "I'm running out of ideas, Eddie."

The man pushed the broom a little more softly and kept his tongue as the Boss's words echoed throughout the place for what seemed like forever. Each time a cube went T-6, the man with the broom would instead wheel out the vacuum. Each time the man would eye the debris while cleaning out the square, and he would mumble, "Too many fingerprints." He waited, always waited for the Boss to ask what he thought. He didn't dare offer words unless asked.

"Softly, Eddie," said the Boss just before he disappeared.

The man did not think it was possible to sweep any more softly, but he tried while remembering the one day he had swept too hard.

He had been pushing his broom past a square for which the clipboard showed its identifier as Aarank 755. Two very bright spheres were moving towards each other. As they grew closer, their relative speed accelerated and their light was blinding yet beautiful. The man knew he wasn't supposed to stop in one area, but he could not look away. As if hypnotized, he relaxed his hands, the broom slipped, and the handle slammed against the hard floor. Dust kicked up. He reached in panic, which somehow made everything appear like slow motion, trying to catch the one, tiny fleck that soared over the railing and into the square. He was about to reach in and grab it, but he remembered the Boss's warning.

He watched the speck as it moved towards the floating spheres that the Boss had so carefully placed. Eventually it touched one small ball and changed its path so very slightly. Its new path gradually took it into the path of another. An incredibly long time later, much more time than the man could perceive, the Boss put a T-6 on the clipboard. Then the man wheeled out the vacuum more slowly than usual.

"Slowly, Eddie," the Boss started saying almost every time he appeared.

It was rare for the man with the broom to be sweeping nearby when the Boss was starting a new project and even more rare for the Boss to invite him to watch. A new grid was opening, a block of nine cubes roped off with the Boss inside the middle cube, like the center of a tic-tac-toe board.

"Thank you, Eddie," he said when the man stopped his broom. There could be no disturbances during a birth. "Would you like to watch?"

"Si," the man said.

"Come, have a seat."

Without lifting a foot, Eddie was suddenly in a chair only an arm's length from the square in which a birth had begun. He watched as the Boss pulled random objects from the pockets of his white jacket, shaped and reshaped them, and placed them at his whim throughout the three dimensions of the cube. Some objects came from the pants pockets, both front and back, each pocket yielding a slightly different color or type of material that he occasionally shaped or mixed with something from another pocket in some way only known to the man in the white suit.

Occasionally, the Boss observed two objects for a length of time and then packed them together to form something new. Some he polished them until they shone, glimmered, or glowed. Some of those would hold their light for a very long time while others might fizzle out before their light could escape the cube, and they would crust over, dull and cloudy.

Too many fingerprints, thought the man in the chair. His bottom lip twitched a distance less than the thickness of a hair in his mustache.

"Yes, Eddie?" asked the Boss.

"No no, Señor."

"You wanted to say something. It's all right. Go ahead."

"No, Señor."

"Eddie, it's okay."

The man looked down, thinking carefully before speaking because it was the first time he could recall the Boss allowing him this close to the birth of a project.

"Señor, what if you took all of those things in your pockets, and you make one big handful, and what if you just toss them into the space?" He waited through uncomfortable silence for the reply that didn't come. "Just toss them in the air?"

The Boss waited. "And then what?"

"Nothing."

"Nothing?"

"Nothing."

The Boss waited. "Why?"

The man spoke the words he had rehearsed many, many times. "Just to see what would happen."

The Boss waited. "Eduardo, nothing would happen."

The man began to sweat. "How do you know, Señor?" The man felt very small. Before he could figure out what to say next, he was back outside the block of nine cubes, broom in hand, and the chair gone. The Boss no longer in front of him, the man with the broom turned and swept in the opposite direction from which he had come.

"Break time, Eddie," said the Boss.

A short time later, or possibly a long time, Eddie was in a chair at a table in a mostly white room. There were no doors, no way in or out, except when the Boss wanted him either in or out. A glass of water appeared in his hand, so he drank as much as he could because he could never be sure when a break would be over or when he might again have a chance for water. He put down the empty glass, but one tiny drop was stuck in the crooked whiskers beneath his nose.

Slowly. Lentamente, Eduardo he thought as he passed a clipboard with identifier "34R+h" across the top of each page. It was a cube that the Boss had checked very recently, so recently that the clipboard was still swinging back and forth on its hook after the Boss had let go of it. On the first page it had "C-1" in the box. In the middle of the cube, at about eye level to Eddie, hung one dark sphere, nothing else. Nothing moved, nothing shone, nothing spun.

As the man pushed the broom past that cube, he heard a very faint "pop," or maybe it was a very loud "pop" because he did not fully know the difference. He turned back and tried to remember if he had ever heard a sound within a cube. What had been a solitary ball had become countless smaller ones. Some glowed, some didn't. Some streaked in circular paths big and small, and some stayed put. Some gathered near others while some remained alone and isolated.

The initial "pop" had caused the man's head to turn so quickly that the tiny drop of water that had stowed away in his mustache had escaped and was now sailing into the cube. Before he was aware of what had happened, it was already too late. Once the drop crossed over the railing to the inside of the square, its flight path went from a gentle arc to a very straight line.

The man's hands began to shake. He instinctively wiped his sleeve across his dry forehead, although he wasn't sure why because he had never done that before. He watched for a long time, or maybe a short time, waiting for an alarm or warning, but nothing happened.

The drop cruised slowly past the outer objects of a cluster, barely missing one with assorted stripes, passing one with a unique ring around it, and drifting close to one that held a red-orange color. They were so close that they leaned towards each other, sensing each other's presence, but they passed too quickly without a chance to meet. The water drop's path was slightly altered by that near encounter, and it wobbled slightly askew and towards a brilliant, pulsing yellow one. Tremendous heat from the yellow one fizzled away some of the moisture in the drop, making it imperceptibly smaller.

Directly beyond the brilliant yellow ball was a rusty brown one that just kind of hung there, right in the line of the drop's motion. The rusty one was about twice the size of the floating drop, and they were on a collision course. A smaller, half silver and half black object with tiny holes also moved towards the rusty one and the drop of water, but then the silvery one kept moving on by and cleared the way for possible impact. The silvery one missed but circled the rusty one and came back around, circling as if on guard, protecting the rusty one. Now, as the drop of water approached, there was a chance it would instead hit the silvery one as it circled the rusty one.

Eddie held his breath as the two objects neared and then touched. The water drop broke into countless tinier drops that stretched away from the object before an invisible force pulled them all back into the rocky orb. There was hissing as a gray fog shrouded the rock. The fog dissipated, leaving the dull rock a little shinier and with a very slight change of its its shape. The man watched as a few cracks opened on its surface, and a red glow began to seep out from inside until it covered the surface. It shaped and reshaped itself, sometimes bubbling and gurgling until another foggy cloud rose above it, enshrining it almost like a silent snowball, gently spinning and gliding amongst the other objects in project "34R+h."

The man reached down for his broom, not sure of how long he had been staring at what he was certain would send the Boss into a verbal explosion. His first thought was to sweep the floor quickly and get out of there, but he could not break from the voice that constantly reminded him to push "slowly." He pushed the broom as far as the next cube before glancing back, but he could no longer see the rusty, cloudy ball. Although there were scattered streaks of white, it had become a beautiful deep blue, a color he could not remember seeing before in any other cube.

The man swept past a few more cubes. He gradually relaxed a bit after each and thought about other things he would never remember until he was startled by the Boss's bellowing voice. "Eddie! Eddie!"

"S-si, Señor," he trembled.

"Eddie! I did it!" The Boss appeared before him, arms raised, one with a fist and one holding the clipboard from 34R+h. "I did it! We got one!"

4. The Accident

*We have all read enough stories about
people who die and become ghosts or
people who have become ghosts but don't
realize they have died. I took that idea and
kind of twisted it a little. Maybe a lot.*

The only thing Jones had been more impressed with
than his new 350-Z two-seater convertible was himself.
For three years he pushed the limits of time and energy,
along with the art of negotiation, strictly for his
promotion and, more importantly, the car. *The* car was
now upside down at the bottom of a small grassy hill off
the right shoulder of Route 295 South.

Jones, from what seemed a comfortable seated
position in tall grass fifty yards from the car, *his* car,
stared in amazement to make certain it really was *his* car
with the wheels pointing skyward like an overturned,
dead turtle. The crowd of emergency personnel made it
more difficult for him to see the platinum-silver car, but
he knew no other reason why he was where he was.

His curiosity, mixed with some concussive effects,
urged him to get closer, and he stumbled through the rest
of the onlookers at the scene. The hairs on his right
forearm prickled up as the breeze from the highway blew
across where his right shirt sleeve used to be. The rest
of the starched white shirt was still on him, along with a
bright red tie, which he loosened as he noticed another
crowd of uniforms gathered around something else – a
body covered with a mostly white sheet. Deep red stains
were soaking through where the head would have been.

On the ground near to the body was a white sleeve from a dress shirt.

"Bastard probably never felt a thing," said a man as he removed his firefighter's helmet.

"Better that way," another replied, "when you don't know it's coming, no time to think. You're just – gone."

Gone. The word echoed in Jones's head and faded like the rush of endless tires on the nearby highway. He stumbled backwards through the tall grass, distancing himself from the voices and flashing lights. He dug his wallet from his left front pocket and reviewed his driver's license just to be sure he was who he was. The faces of his wife and kids all matched his memory as did his name and picture, and he put it all back in his pocket while taking further steps towards the woods behind him. He turned and picked up speed until he reached a full sprint, which lasted for only a few seconds before he slowed without breath. He dropped to one knee before curling in a fetal position and sobbing beneath the frozen arms of a family of oak trees whose spring buds were days away from exploding. When he pulled his hands from his face a minute later, he noticed blood and thought of the sheet over the body back at the accident scene.

He leapt to his feet, hands away from his body as if his own blood might contaminate him. His eyes darted until they found the shimmer of a stream, then he walked almost ape-like across a grassy opening in the trees until reaching a bend of a tributary that strayed from the Delaware River about ten miles west. Jones squatted, thrashing his bloody hands in the ripples before allowing the water to calm to reveal his matted hair, but he saw no source of the blood. That concerned him more than the blood.

He felt a wave of panic that reached back to the men at the crash site, the sheet covering the body with the bloody head, his missing sleeve next to the sheet, and the comfort in the suggestion that maybe he never felt a thing. After his shoulders relaxed, he stepped knee-deep into the stream and bent forward to rinse his hair, and wash his thoughts about death.

"I guess I get to keep my body. Good thing I never filled out that donor card." He chuckled, forcing a smile. "But why would I need my body? Wouldn't I just be more like a spirit? Is there a reason I'm still physical? Or maybe I just appear physical to me. What about-"

His thoughts stopped abruptly when he glanced up to the short bridge that spanned the stream. Standing beside a blue and white '67 Mustang on the bridge was a frail man about half his age. His greasy, unkempt hair shone in the sun as his ultra-pale arm reached out of a t-shirt and attempted a timid wave at Jones.

"Hey!" he yelled, as if a plane was circling his island. The young man seemed startled and moved toward the driver's side door. "Hey, wait up!" The skinny man bent as if to enter the car, then paused, looked each way down and up the road, bent again, stood again, and waited as Jones traversed the stream and climbed up a small embankment to the bridge. He approached the man cautiously while catching his breath.

"Hi. You can see me?"

"Y-yeah. I just didn't expect that you'd see me." The young man had imperfect teeth that were never totally covered by his closed mouth. His arms reached across his abdomen as he sort of hugged himself.

"I just had sort of a problem with my car, and I don't think it turned out too well," Jones explained.

"Looks to me like you made it okay," the man smiled. "I'm Glen," and he slowly extended his hand, as did Jones.

"Jones. Well, my name is David, but I got tired of the 'Davy Jones locker' jokes, so I just go by Jones." He touched his head again, checking for more blood. "I know I'm babbling, but, I mean, I had this new car, and there was this accident, I think, and it seemed like nobody could see me back there."

"I know what you mean," Glen laughed. "It took me a long time to get used to that, but I guess I'm still not used to it. C'mon. Get in." They did, and Glen drove off.

"So how long, I mean, well, I'm not sure what to ask. I mean, I got like a million questions, I don't know where to start."

"Really?"

"Yeah, I mean. Can people see us? Do they see you?"

Glen half laughed and shrugged. "They see the car, kind of stare at it actually, but they don't see me. I thought the car would help, but it doesn't."

"Sorry to hear that." Jones assessed the man's clothes and demeanor before figuring him for a suicide victim, which curbed his next question. "Are there others like – like us?"

"A handful. That's where I'm going now."

"Can I come?"

Glen looked carefully at Jones while trying to watch the road and fighting off a smile. "Sure. They'll be glad to meet you."

"Who's 'they'?"

"Just some friends. More people who the rest of the world doesn't see." As they drove, Jones noticed what seemed like a jagged scar still healing on Glen's left wrist and filled in the blank for the question he never asked.

Glen eventually pulled into a gravel driveway of a massive, gray Victorian house with several small lightning rods reaching up from the top of two onion dome turrets on each front corner of the three-story house.

As Jones stepped from the car, he craned his head upward and said, "I've driven down this road a hundred times, but don't ever remember seeing this house before.

"Sometimes we don't notice something until we need it," answered Glen.

"Who lives here?" Jones looked around the area, trying to place other landmarks with the house, but nothing at all looked familiar even though he drove the road at least once a week.

"Nobody really *lives* here," answered Glen. "We just come here when we need to, or when we aren't sure where we belong. Or sometimes just for support."

"Oh," Jones jumped in. "support, like, what to do and what are there rules or anything? Are there certain things we're supposed to do, or things we're not supposed to do?"

Glen paused, taking his hand from the doorknob. "Rules are kind of arbitrary. It's just like everywhere else really. Golden Rule kind of stuff. Don't do what you wouldn't want anyone to do to you. It's really universal, even here." They went in.

Jones didn't realize what a brilliantly sunny day it was until he swam into the darkness inside. He closed his eyes to help his pupils adjust, and he soon saw a group sitting around a quiet living room. He baby-stepped into a circle of seven chairs of various styles, each chair filled with someone barely visible in the darkness, all sitting silent and straight. One chair was empty, which Jones assumed belonged to Glen, and one chair was much larger than the others. That chair was against a large window on the far side of the room. He could see the outline of a woman in shadow, like the dark side of the moon as the sun smacked her from behind. Glen approached her and whispered while the other shadowed heads turned and followed him.

"Welcome, Mr. Jones," said a solemn and aged woman. "Glen tells me that you have many questions. I'm assuming you've had what some people call a - *change of life*."

Jones nodded. "I guess you could call it that."

"Perhaps we can be of some help. Please have a seat and let's talk." He could not recall a voice that had ever filled him with such comfort, as if he could ask the most obvious or insane question, make a completely ludicrous statement, and he'd hear only praise.

"Take *my* seat," said Glen, pointing to the empty chair directly opposite the woman. Jones moved for it, sorting his thoughts and nodding to the others while sitting like the new guy at a board meeting. Glen stood beside the woman in shadow. "Mr. Jones waved to me today. It was nice to be noticed," Glen offered to the group, and they immediately turned heads towards each other, to Glen, the woman for her response, and then Jones.

"Forgive me, Mr. Jones. My name is Mary." Jones guessed Mary to be approaching 90 but couldn't be sure because of the velvety voice and awkward lighting. All he could be sure about was that she had hair, was short, and smiled when she spoke.

"I have a few questions, if you don't mind."

"Of course you do, Mr. Jones. We all do. That's why we're here."

"That's the first one. *Where* is *here*? And is *here* a – a *good* place?"

"Yes, Mr. Jones, this is the best place, but it's just that. A place, one of many. Sometimes we're finished in one place. We move on to another. Sometimes we know exactly where the next place is. Sometimes we're not sure. Some of us find places like this to stay awhile, talk with others who are moving on, and decide where to go next."

"So we have choices? It's not like we're told where to go or we get taken away somewhere?"

"Some of us get taken away, but that would have happened by now so I'm sure you're fine. We always have choices, but poor choices are hard to reverse and always leave an emotional mark. It helps to talk to others and move on together when possible."

Jones paused, still barely able to see anyone's face. "Was it unusual that I saw Glen today? I mean, can people see me?"

Mary placed her hand upon Glen's as it rested on the arm of her chair. "Most people do not really *see* us, not the way we'd like to be seen. Most people look right through us, but if they really want to, they can see and talk to us just like they'd talk to their own brother or sister, or child or best friend. We can all see each other, and it's not difficult for us to find others just like us. We're everywhere, moving about the world just like everyone else."

"I feel hungry. Is that normal?"

"Most of us don't feel hungry very often," she leaned forward and smiled, "but I would say it's a sign of progress for you."

"Do I stay here a certain amount of time? Do I know when to go or do you tell me when? Is there anything I have to do or something I have to know?"

"Mr. Jones, you're probably not going to like this answer, and I completely understand, but there are no signs. There's nothing to tell us when or where to go. When *you* feel like the time is right, you go. When *you* feel that you know where to go, you go. So many have come here expecting answers or expecting to be told to go here, go there, do this or that, but it really is up to you. I can help you sort through the choices and priorities, but nobody can tell you *when* you are ready or *where* you should go."

Jones looked to the floor, then up again. "I'd like to go see my family."

Mary sat back in her chair. "It might be too soon for that. It would probably be very upsetting to you and to them as well."

"So they'll see me?"

- 59 -

"Yes, *you* they will certainly see. They might not see Glen or the rest of us, but they'll see you. Unless you don't want to be seen. There are things we can do to avoid that, and I'm sure Glen can help you. Sometimes we naturally gravitate towards others, and the fact that you were found by Glen tells me that you should probably stick together for a while." She looked up at him and patted his hand. "Glen is more intelligent than even he is aware. He's had his life trampled, but he's recovering just fine."

"Are there any rules I need to know?"

"Some rules are moral or religious based, like marriage. Some are common sense, like stealing. Do everything just as you always did."

"So we can have possessions?"

"We can *all* have possessions," she smiled, "but don't focus on them. As for rules, the only rule here is the Golden Rule."

Thoughts were sinking into Jones, crawling through his veins. Acceptance was first, flooding through him like slipping into a hot bath, but he wasn't sure if he was ready for the bath, ready to accept a new, different existence.

"I sense some hesitation, Mr. Jones," Mary said.

"This is just so sudden. I mean, I didn't have a chance to-. Last night I go to bed, kiss my wife good night, and everything was normal. Then – everything gets ripped out from under you."

"It is good you feel that way. We all get here in different ways, for different reasons. None are good, just different. The important part is not what got us here but what we do from this point forward. I understand that you want to see her, and so would I if I were you. Give it time. Give *her* time."

"It's the suddenness. I just wasn't ready."

"And some people would say you're lucky for that. There are some of us who go through months and years of therapy and medications and failure. Tears, waking up with nightmares, knowing that the inevitable is going to catch up with you. Trying to figure out what to say to your partner, not knowing how to say goodbye, but you know that you eventually have to say one last goodbye. And sometimes, with no mercy, it happens and it's over just as quickly as it started. Some of us would have gladly had your experience instead of theirs."

When Jones stood, Glen pulled his hand away from Mary and walked behind his chair to put a hand on his new friend's shoulder.

"You two should go outside and talk," suggested Mary, and they did.

The sunlight was painful to his eyes as they left the darkness of the house, and Jones wondered, briefly, why Glen didn't seem to be affected. "I guess you're used to everything."

"Not yet, but I'm getting there."

Jones braced his palms on the railing of the wrap-around porch about fifty feet from the county road where intermittent traffic regularly exceeded the speed limit, slowing only when approaching a bend in the road. "Are there other places like this?" he asked. "Other places I could have gone?"

"Sure," Glen said, "but this is the first one I found."

"You been here long?" Jones turned and sat on the railing, looking toward Glen who now sat in one of several rocking chairs.

"A few weeks. I spent about a year just wandering around, kept thinking I could just handle it myself and didn't need anyone else, but it kind of got boring. Then I found out about Mary, and I'm just about ready to get out of here."

"Where you going?"

"Don't know yet, maybe cross the country, see places I never saw before. Maybe meet some others."

"Can I go with you?" Jones asked while standing off the railing.

"Sure," said Glen with an ambivalent smile.

"Let's go. Now. Today." Jones's enthusiasm grew.

"N-now? L-let me check with Mary first, because-"

"What for? She said we'll know when we're ready. You said you're ready, and I don't want to sit around here waiting."

"Yeah, but you might need some time. I mean, this all happened to you just this morning."

"Yeah, but you've been through all this, and I'm sure you can help me with the tough parts. Let's just get in the car and go."

"*My* car?"

"We sure can't use mine," laughed Jones as they walked toward the Mustang in the gravel driveway. "Don't worry. If you get tired, I'll drive for a while. How do you pay for the gas?" Jones asked. "I mean, do you just hand them a credit card?"

"My wife maxxed out my cards," Glen said.

"Her problem now, right?" Glen's frown caught Jones' attention. "Hey, I'm sorry. That was kind of insensitive of me. I wasn't thinking, but don't worry about paying for anything. I'll hit a few ATM's and we'll be fine." He patted his left hand on Glen's right shoulder, not bringing him back to a smile but at least neutralizing the frown. "Can we go past my house?"

"You heard Mary. It's probably too soon."

"Yeah, but who knows when we'll be back this way? Just for a few minutes. How about this? We get there, you watch the clock. One minute and we're outta there, no matter what, no arguments, nothing. Even if I argue, you just drive us away."

"You sure? No arguments?"

"Swear to God. I guess that means a little more now than it did yesterday."

"One thing Mary wants us to realize is that we can help ourselves a lot more than trying to lean on God." Glen got in his side of the car, reached across, and unlocked the other door for Jones to get in. "It's not like God doesn't listen. He does, if that's your faith, and he can help us feel more at peace with ourselves. But it's not like he can reach down and actually touch or change anything."

"Mary said that?" asked Jones.

"Yep."

"I guess she's the authority, right? Is she, like, *connected* in some way, or is she just one of us?"

"She's kind of in charge. I know she said that we can all go when we're ready, but she really decides that.

One guy just wouldn't listen, so she sent him away, told him he's not allowed to be here anymore."

"Sent him away? Where?"

"Not sure."

"I didn't know she had that kind of power."

Glen started the car. "It's *her* house."

———————————————

A light rain fell. Beads of water dotted the windows and body of the well-waxed Mustang like tiny bubbles. Jones's house was on the corner of a quiet, rural development on what had been farmland up until two years ago. They parked four houses away, which would have been more like the distance of eight houses in a residential neighborhood in most towns. The driveway was full of cars and a few in front of the house, including one police car.

"These people got here fast. The blue Corvette is my cousin David's. The white minivan is my sister-in-law's. That silver one I'm not sure, might be one of my wife's friends. The pick-up truck is my brother's. Not sure about the Cadillac. I hate Cadillacs."

"One minute," said Glen.

"Get closer."

"Not good, especially with a cop there."

"What's that got to do with it?"

"If she sees you with a cop there, that could be trouble. You really *are* new at this."

Jones cracked an internal smile as he pictured his wife being led away in a straight jacket by men in white coats. Although he would never wish any pain upon his family, he certainly expected his wife to be rather distraught given the circumstances.

"Okay, let's get out of here. If I see my kids, I might fall apart."

"Good thinking. You'll have plenty of time to see them later."

"Really?"

"Of course," Glen said with a comforting voice. "Those things get worked out later. Right now, the important part is understanding that you're here, she's there, and that's the way it's going to be. Accept it and move on."

"I'm working on that, and I'm hungry too," Jones added. "Make a right out of the development. There's a farm stand down the road. I need a banana and an apple."

The Mustang stopped at a wagon big enough to be pulled by a tractor. A steel box with a slot in the top sat inside a milk crate for courteous folks to drop money in and take apples, tomatoes, bananas, cucumbers, and whatever else the farmer offered. The farmer made the bulk of his money selling to the local supermarkets, but he also gained a few extra bucks with the roadside stand. Jones dropped a dollar in and took two apples and two bananas, one each for Glen and himself, then they headed east with no specific location just yet.

"So what's the biggest change, the biggest difference that you've noticed?" asked Jones. "I mean, so far, nothing is really any different for me as far as I can tell. And I'm kind of freaked that I can actually eat."

"Biggest thing for me at first was how much I appreciated little things even more. I'd drive by a school

- 65 -

bus, see a line of kids on their way to school, and I'd break down. Or I'd see a couple out for a walk, holding hands, and that would do me in. The mall at Christmas time, *before* – I hated it just because of the crowds. Now I miss it. I miss not buying things for someone special. I can't even remember what Christmas Spirit feels like."

"Spirit," said Jones. "That's funny."

"If I could, I'd probably sleep from Christmas Eve, right through past New Year's Day."

"Hey, I didn't think about that. Do you sleep? There must be a ton of little things I haven't even thought about yet."

"You'll have many sleepless nights, for sure," Glen said. "But don't focus on that. Focus on the free time. Going where you want, when you want, like right now. If you want to turn the stereo up at midnight, then do it. Or if you want to hang in a bar until closing time, no problem. Who's going to yell at you when you get home?"

"Do we even *have* homes? Do we *need* them?"

"Depends on what you mean by a *home*. We do, but it'll be more like a *house*, not a *home* anymore. You'll feel in transition for a while. You'll take whatever you can find at first, then you'll want to move up."

"Up? Oh, right. I was wondering when that happens."

"The important thing right now is to have fun with it and do whatever you can to put a smile on your face, without hurting anyone else of course. Take advantage of whatever you can while you can. Stretch limits. Push them. After a while, you'll get tired of that and you'll want to settle yourself down again, figure out where you are, what got you here, and what it all means. Why it happened. Once you understand the *why* part, then you'll relax about it. You can't change it, so just make the best of it. Look forward, not backward."

Jones removed his tie as Glen's words gained emotional momentum. He reached out with the tie, letting it flap in the air current around the car. As they passed three teenagers walking along the road, he let go of the tie and watched as the kids turned their heads as the tie settled on the side of the road. Jones and Glen looked at each other with a quiet laugh.

"Stop at the library, up at the next traffic light," Jones ordered.

"Library?"

"Yeah. Just follow me and stay quiet." After the Mustang roared into the parking lot, Glen followed Jones into the brick building. "Don't say anything. Just stand back, watch people, and then follow me."

They walked in a fraction after the automatic doors opened for someone walking out. Jones stepped softly as he passed the elderly librarian behind the main desk on his right. He moved to the reference section beyond the foyer and began to remove encyclopedias from a shelf. One by one, he stacked them in the middle of the floor. The few patrons in that area watched as book after book reached higher and higher. Glen did as he was told, stepping back further as others stepped closer.

When Jones was satisfied with the height of the books, he held one by the front and back covers, pages hanging below, and flapped the covers as if a heavy paper bird was flying across the room, back towards the front door. Jones's smile increased as more and more speechless people kept their eyes on the flapping book.

"Mr. Rubin," called the librarian, "could you come see this, sir?" Jones played along, allowing the book to hover a few seconds near her desk before moving toward the exit.

"Pretty crazy," Mr. Rubin said.

"Should I call somebody?" she asked.

"Yes, but don't touch any books. It might be evidence of something."

Jones brought the book down on her desk, placing it so it stood tent-like before her. As she picked up the phone, Mr. Rubin grabbed a pencil and paper, making notes quickly as Jones motioned to Glen that it was time to leave.

"Did you see their faces?" Jones exploded as they reached the car "That was the craziest thing I ever did!"

Glen's eyebrows shifted, "I'm sure 'crazy' is pretty much what they were thinking too, but let's not make a habit of that, okay?"

"You're the one who said to take advantage and have fun with it."

"Not exactly what I meant." They drove only a few minutes before Jones burst again.

"Hey, pull in this parking lot. The supermarket." Glen did so with reluctance, pulling into a space near a shopping cart corral as Jones stumbled out of the car before it came to a complete stop. "C'mon."

Immediately inside was the produce section. Jones walked up to the apples and grabbed three. Each time a shopper pushed a cart within reach, he dropped an apple into the cart and enjoyed the confused eyes on the shoppers as they sped away and tossed the apples into boxes of oranges, onions, and whatever else was around.

Jones took three more apples and stood in the middle of the produce area, his smile growing as shoppers slowed down with the feeling that something unusual was about to happen. Jones looked at Glen before tossing one, then two, then three apples in the air, keeping them aloft with a typical juggling pattern. Jones's eyes danced from the fruit to his audience and back as Glen moved close enough to whisper. "I think someone's getting the manager. C'mon, let's get out of here."

"I'm just having fun, like you said."

"I said have as much fun as you can but not at the expense of others. Let's get out of here before there is trouble."

"Trouble. From who?" Jones laughed.

"Whoever is in charge."

"I don't think he's really gonna care about a few apples."

"Probably not, but he'll care about scaring customers away."

"Fine. Let's go." On the way out, Jones place two apples back in the basket and began eating the third. Speechless people watched as Jones held the apple up, moved it left, right, and in a circle, loving that everyone else's attention followed the moving apple.

Glen had run to the car and pulled in front of the store. As Jones hopped into the car, a balding man in a starched shirt and tie scribbled notes on an index card, glancing between the card and the car until it was beyond his sight.

_____

An hour later they had crossed the Walt Whitman Bridge and reached the other side of Philadelphia where the buildings were smaller and trees bigger.

"You hungry?" asked Jones. "I'm hungry. I didn't think I'd be hungry."

"You just had apples and a banana."

"I know, but do you think it means something?"

"I barely ate at first," said Glen. "Lost a lot of weight, but I started eating normal after a week."

"I need a burger. You want one?"

"No, I'm good."

Glen pulled into a rest area along I-76 and said, ""I'll wait out here."

"Sure you don't want anything?"

"Nope. Take your time." Glen reclined the seat and hoped to take a short nap.

Jones approached the doors of the rest area. In front of him was a woman in her mid-20's pushing a stroller containing a comfortable and quiet child, who Jones didn't notice because his attention was glued to one of the shortest skirts he could remember seeing other than on a website. Cro-Magnon Jones followed her right to the counter where she ordered two cheeseburgers and fries. He stood in awe with a little lust, and it didn't take long for him to realize that he didn't have to ask Glen if physical reactions to sexual urges were going to be any different. He stood very close behind her as she waited for her food and tried to smell her perfume without making any noise or touching her. He had been thinking about Glen's words regarding scaring people, and he did not want to frighten a mother pushing an infant in a stroller.

He stepped back and leaned a little to the right, trying to answer what burned his curiosity, but he couldn't lean over far enough. He got down on his knees, peering beneath her skirt, and then he had his answer. He fought the urge to step into the ladies room and fulfill a high school fantasy when a distraction arrived in the form of a hefty teenager with four double-cheeseburgers on a tray on his way to a seat. The boy put the tray down as he grabbed a cup for soda and took it a few steps around a corner to fill it with Mountain Dew. Upon his return, only three cheeseburgers remained. One, half-eaten, was on its way out the door.

"Wake up, Buddy," Jones said, climbing into the car and disturbing the sleep that Glen had not yet reached. "Ever been to Chicago?"

"No."

"You like pizza?"

"Of course," he answered as he sparked the engine back to life.

"Then you'll like Chicago."

They left the parking lot and only needed a few seconds for the Mustang to reach 70, at which Glen enabled the cruise control. About ten minutes down the highway a Pennsylvania State Trooper rushed the opposite way towards the rest area they had just left.

"You mind if I take a nap? It's been a strange day," Jones said as he reclined the seat and folded his arms over his eyes. "Once I get a little sleep, I'll be able to better understand what you've been trying to tell me about everything. I'm sure I've been pretty annoying today."

"I got the radio if I need company," Glen said as Jones drifted away quickly, rocked to sleep by the moving vehicle despite the wind rushing around him.

An hour later Jones jumped up in his seat, startled, looking at Glen with initial surprise as he tried to remember why he was in someone else's sports car speeding along a highway surrounded by green hills dotted with cows. The whole day quickly ran back to him like a wave rolling up a beach before sizzling and sinking into the sand.

"You okay?" Glen asked.

"Yeah, sure," stammered Jones as he struggled to open his eyes against the sunset that sliced through the windshield of the westbound car. "I just kind of forgot everything for a while, and then it all came rushing back to me."

"Yeah, that'll happen. Feels great for a few seconds, then it feels like hell all over again." Glen allowed him half a minute before continuing. "So you think you want to hang out for a while?"

"Where else am I gonna go?"

"There are lots of divorce groups," said Glen "but I think you should stick with Mary. She really knows how to help. Always knows exactly the right thing to say in those tough times, and believe me – you've got some tough times ahead of you."

A song was fading out as a news announcer cut in. "Police in New Jersey have yet to find the driver of a vehicle involved in an accident earlier today. At about noon a car registered to David Jones of Montford, New

Jersey, went off the road at mile 47 of Route 295 South. A body was found at the scene, a male in his 40's, but the identification on that body matched that of the owner of a disabled vehicle found roughly a half mile away. Police believe the man had been walking along the highway when he was struck and killed by the sports car owned by Jones. Although Jones has not been found, witnesses said an unidentified male was seen walking away from the wreckage. Police are withholding the identity of the man struck and killed pending notification of his family."

Jones sat up. Police sirens caught his attention as a Pennsylvania State Trooper approached from behind. The radio announcer continued. "And I'm now being told that someone matching the description of Jones was seen vandalizing a library, shoplifting from a supermarket, and looking up a teenage girl's skirt in a fast food restaurant." The announcer chuckled. "I tell you, it doesn't get much weirder than that. Warm and sunny today with a high of 84 degrees, and that's what's happening."

In addition to flipping his car, vomiting in a moving convertible was another new experience for Jones that day.

5. White Cotton

*Heidi Sieverding is a published author who
writes what I call "sexy horror," a
combination of romance and devilish
creatures. She asked me to write something
to post on her blog. I don't write about
devilish creatures, but I can write about sexy
people who end up in unusual situations.
And just when you think it has gotten
unusual, it goes a little further.*

"Don't get attached."

"It's just sex."

"Don't take anything personally."

"You're just an actor, pretending to be someone
else."

"Think of it as working out at the gym or
cheerleading practice."

There were other things Jess had told Marti a year
ago about becoming as an escort. Grades in college
were not as good as they should have been, and there
was no time to work even if a part-time job was
available.

"Luckily, men in college towns have a lot of college
money, and they are willing to pay for college students.
Trust me," Jess said, "wealthy, middle-aged men do a lot
of things you would not expect them to do. It'll be fine.
They're all tested, and they're all traceable if something
happens. They won't hurt you, but *you will* hurt them

They are going to want you. They are going to tell you they will dump their wives for you. It never happens, almost never, but you want to make them say it anyway. It means they will be back, and their wallets will open a little further each time. And so will you."

When bills were mounting, it was important to simplify. Out at clubs, Jess was always paying, until the pride was swallowed and Marti could not contain her question. Jess said, "You have no idea how long I've been waiting for you to ask. Let's get out of here, and I'll tell you all about it." Marti had never seen Jess with so big a smile.

"No friggin' way!" Marti said.

"Swear to God."

"How can you do that?"

"I said the same thing, and it was way easier than I thought. All the work is done for you. You just show up, there are so many clothes and outfits to choose from. Ms. Coven, the boss, she'll buy you whatever you want. Most of the time the customers tell you what to wear anyway. You just might have to grease yourself up a little. It's all safe, all protected. It's far enough out of town. You won't see any of the stupid college boys from around here because they'd never be able to afford you. You might see their fathers though, and every once in a while, the mothers. They usually come two at a time, so you can't be shy. And please keep this in mind. They only take beautiful people. If you weren't pretty enough, I would not have told you all this."

The rent cost for room 6I at the Ivy Arms was easily covered by the income. Ms. Coven had the only key and the only list of names, both staff and clients. As far as anyone in the building knew, a nice, older woman, a doctor, lived very quietly and had occasional business partners for daytime meetings. If something went wrong, she had her explanation solid. "It's not prostitution. This nice couple hired me as a sex therapist."

It was a small, two-bedroom suite for which Ms. Coven's rent was reduced because of the renovations she financed, specifically the master bathroom with the double vanity, garden tub, double-sized grotto shower with cushioned benches, and heat lamps. If any staff or client did not shower both before and after a session, it would be the last time either would set foot in the apartment. Many clients just could not wait and wanted their session to begin with the shower, often ending there as well.

The second bedroom was Ms. Coven's secure office. It was simply furnished and mainly served as a place where occasionally Ms. Coven would hide, listen, and sometimes watch transactions through hidden cameras and microphones. She was smart enough to leave nothing directly connected to her in the apartment, which was actually rented by a company called "Behavioral Health Associates," which was nothing more than a post office box on the other side of the city. She had a degree in social science and the credentials to claim to title "therapist."

When Ms. Coven met Marti, she was so pleased that she gave Jess double the usual recruiting bonus. In the envelope with the money was a note that said, "This one is going to break hearts." After the first year, a few hearts had been broken, but Marti's was one of them.

In apartment 6I, staff had their own armoire with their favorite "gift wrappings." That's what Ms. Coven called their lingerie and accessories such as blindfolds, handcuffs, toys, lotions, etc. She supplied them with anything they needed, and anything they needed was theirs alone without any sharing. Safer that way. Ms. Coven was willing to spend up front because trends had shown that investments in this business eventually more than paid for themselves.

"Yes, Ms. Coven," Marti said. "I know. I've had this type before. I can handle it."

After a shower and a peek at the clock, the armoire that read "Marti" opened. "I've had this type before," was said again silently, but then Marti remembered saying those same words months ago. The voice mail that day said he was wealthy but shy, and if all went well, this one would want Marti all to himself, exclusively, and he'd be able to pay the extra easily and regularly. Memories of him brought Marti to reach for just the right item in the armoire: the tailored, white dress shirt the shy man had left behind all those months ago. Marti's eyes closed while buttoning, then unbuttoning. Memories of how he had unbuttoned it in front of Marti. The man's fingers were unable to coordinate, twice getting buttons out of sequence, but Marti loved how vulnerable it made him look.

Jess had warned her that some girls had gotten too attached, believing they'll convince guys to dump their wives for them and save them from this job. Jess had done it once, and it did not end well. Nor had it ended well for Marti.

The white cotton shirt sitting on the bed was a memory of one of their more special times. He had a weekend conference in Florida and flew Marti down, had a car waiting, and they enjoyed the pool and beach before and after meetings. They sat in the bar at lunch and pretended to have just met. They dined at a restaurant away from the conference hotel and pretended to have just met. They danced at exclusive clubs a cab ride away and pretended to have just met. Marti didn't love it but liked it a lot. Didn't love or like him, but it was somewhere between and changing a little each time they were together, despite Jess's warning.

They spent hours together in Marti's room each night, hours including the balcony, the elevator, the stairs, the sauna, the parking lot, and near the pool. It was sad that he always had to return to his room in case one of the other associates was looking for him or his wife called. Once, as he was dressing again, he pulled his shirt on more easily than the first time when he had fumbled with the buttons. Marti crept up behind him, reached beneath his arms, and unbuttoned it.

"Hey," he smiled, "I have to go."

"But you can leave this with me."

He turned, smiled, and kissed Marti on the forehead before leaving. Marti slept in his shirt that night and many other nights. The material felt perfect, such soft cotton. Even on a hanger, his shoulders, pects, and biceps seemed to still be inside. It perfectly matched him. It *was* him, and it was not easy to give in and wash it, wash away the smell of him.

"Custom made," he said. "I have a few dozen of them. Gifts from my wife." Then he left, but never came back again. No notes, no explanations, no apologies. He left Marti a plane ticket to return home, and cars had been arranged at both ends. Marti waited, hoping to see him in the airport lounge and pretending to have just met. Acting classes had taught Marti the art of small talk, but now Marti just felt small.

On this day, with this new client, Marti needed to erase his memory from the shirt. No buttons were fastened. Completely open, the collar and the whole shirt pulled wide, everything exposed. "I've had this type before," echoed in Marti's head. A glass of cocoanut rum over ice slid down easily, which was well into taking effect when there was a knock. Ms. Coven's assistant answered, searched the client for anything not permitted in apartment 6I of the Ivy Arms, and then he excused himself. The client followed the previously reviewed directions and headed for the shower where there were towels and a stocked liquor cabinet. Vodka over ice, then a shower, then dressed in something special before returning to the living room that was darker than before.

Marti, with nothing but the white dress shirt and another glass of rum, walked softly in bare feet from the bedroom into the living room where the client stood admiring a soft leather arm chair. The client saw Marti, smiled, and stood before the leather chair. Bare feet were requested because it seemed submissive. This one liked that. "This one," said Ms. Coven, "has a strong hand. You sure you can take a little pain?" Marti laughed. "I know pain."

Marti walked slowly, feigning shyness, but admiring the long legs in black thigh-hi stockings, 4-inch heels, a black leather vest, and a black thong with what seemed like diamonds in the front. The tall woman smiled down at Marti, extending a hand and taking one back. She ran her older hands along Marti's forearm to a small bicep

- 79 -

until the rolled up sleeve of the white dress shirt stopped her. The tall woman opened the shirt and put her soft hands around Marti's waist, pulling closer for a soft kiss.

Just a person, Marti repeated *who needs attention. Enjoy it. Enjoy giving someone pleasure. She just wants to borrow you and will pay very well for it. Close your eyes and just enjoy the warmth of a mouth on your neck and forget it's a woman.* Marti learned to enjoy being pulled close, hands running across a soft leather vest and the softer D cup breasts spilling out. What had Ms. Coven said about this one?

She was angry. After years of wondering, she finally stopped asking her husband if he had cheated on her. There were always questionable things, and his answers were never convincing. She told her husband that she would never question him again. She would be the quiet wife and play along, smile at parties, kiss him in public to protect the assets, but she was going to have her own fun. She was going to find her own "toys." She would become another man's "toy." For a while it was one. Then two, eventually three, and eventually she realized that something more was needed. She enjoyed giving up herself to the power of others, but today was going to be different. She didn't like her pain. Today, she was bringing pain to someone else, pretending to bring it to her husband. It was her turn, and she was making the most of it. Her playing hurt him more than his playing had hurt her because she was the mother of his children. For some reason, it was different. All those years of spoiling him, giving him everything, but now she was spoiling herself. Giving herself to whoever she wanted, and taking whoever she wanted.

She put a finger beneath Marti's chin, lifted, and feasted on the exposed, vulnerable neck. One hand found Marti's curly hair. Her fingers wrapped into the brunette locks that she pulled back to show even more neck to feed on. Marti had trouble remembering it was just a job. The woman's lips and tongue found the perfect spot behind Marti's ear. Knees weakened. The woman sensed that and guided Marti to kneel, then she stood with her legs apart. Marti had not felt this good in a long time. Not since Florida. Marti had been toughened, but it was time to let it go.

Again, the woman's fingers locked in Marti's hair, and she felt warm kisses exactly where she wanted to be kissed. The tall woman sat in the leather chair, draped her legs over each arm, and pulled Marti closer. Her hands worked their way to Marti's neck, massaging tense muscles as both grew hungrier. The woman pushed back the collar of Marti's white dress shirt, exposing soft shoulders that begged to be kissed. That's when she stopped.

The woman sat up, heels on the floor, and pushed the white dress shirt off Marti's arms. Marti reached up and began to pull off the woman's thong. Eyes, hunger, and pulse growing, and fumbling hands pulling the thong down for the woman to step out of, but those tall heels remained planted on the floor. Marti looked up, unsure what was wrong.

The woman, now standing over Marti, had a curious expression. She looked down and asked, "Young man, where did you get this shirt?"

6. The Lie

*There have been too many stories, mainly
movies, involving the telling of lies. As
stated with other stories in this collection, I
did not want to write what has already been
written unless I could put a significant twist
into it. Here was have, as we have had
before, a society in which lying has not
existed. What separates mine from others is
that I go further with what repercussions
might surface once the concept has been
figured out.*

George couldn't see that he was sweating, but he felt
the line of moisture trace its way down the side of his
head. It curved slightly at his jawbone then ducked
behind his jowl towards his neck. It only increased as
Mrs. Irwin got closer, striding up and down each aisle of
her 7th grade classroom. He glanced two seats ahead at
his best friend Eric who, as usual, was sketching fighter
jets in the margins of his notebook.

"And George, your homework?"

His eyes tightened, then relaxed slightly. "No, Mrs.
Irwin."

Her shoulders dropped. "Again? What's going on?"

"I'm really sorry. I was just getting started last
night, and then my dad said to take the dog for a walk.
His collar came loose, and he ran off. And then we
spent all night looking for him." George tried to peek up
at his teacher but couldn't. "By the time we got home, I

forgot all about the math homework. I'm really sorry."
He braced himself for what he could not imagine.

"Well, I'm glad the dog was okay, but please make
up the assignment tonight." Eyes tight, he listened as
her shoes clicked along the wood floor to the next
student. His head dropped, arms relaxed, and chest
exhaled.

Hours later he paced the dry sidewalk as Eric tried to
keep pace. "Hey," Eric said, "George, are you listening
to anything I'm saying?"

"Sorry." George slowed, blinking as if he had just
sat up in bed.

"What's wrong? I've known you since before
kindergarten. I know when something's wrong. What's
going on?" George looked around, noticing they were
across the street from the town park in the center of
Edenton in the state of Illinois. He then nodded for Eric
to follow him until they stopped beneath a gathering of
trees.

"Remember when Irwin was walking around
checking math homework?" George whispered.

"Yeah. Why are you whispering?"

"Remember when I told her why I didn't have my
homework done?"

"No," said Eric. "Your hands are shaking. You
sick? You're all sweaty."

"I told her I didn't have my homework because the
dog ran away," he fought to catch his breath. "Then by
the time we found the dog, I forgot all about doing my
homework."

"Okay, so you do it tonight and you get half credit,
like usual. What's the big deal?"

George inhaled sharply. "That's not what happened."

"What do you mean?"

"The story with the dog. Didn't happen."

Eric tried to focus. "I don't under-"

"It didn't happen!" George yelled. "I told her something that was not – not real. Not right." George walked in a tight circle.

"But – I don't understand. Why would you say something like that? You can't. I mean, it – I – I never – really? Something that did not actually happen? But- you told it to her as if it *did* happen? If it didn't happen, why'd you say it?"

"I don't know. It just came out. I don't understand either."

"I never knew you could do that. That anyone could do that. This doesn't make sense. I mean, it *does*, but it doesn't. Have you thought about this? Where did you even get an idea to try something like that?"

"It just popped out. I couldn't help it," George cried. "It would have been the third assignment I missed this week. I was afraid of getting punished by my dad, detention after school, who knows what else." George wiped at his eyes. "I told her about the dog so I wouldn't get in trouble again."

Eric straightened up as his eyes widened. "You told her stuff that's not – real? This is like something from another planet." They both dropped their backpacks into a small crush of fall leaves. "Do you have any idea what you've done?" Eric ran both hands through his curly hair. "This – this is something like science fiction. This could throw the world into spinning the wrong way or something."

"I don't know how it happened. It just came to me. She was at Terry's desk behind me, and I was getting all nervous. Then she asked me for my homework," he paused, wiping his eyes again, "and it just blurted out."

"Well, IT didn't just blurt out. YOU blurted it out."

"I know, I know," George whined. "I don't know what to do. Help me think."

Eric shook his head. "Dude, you're a great friend and all, but this might be too much. I mean, we have no idea what could happen," he glanced around at the streets that surrounded the park, "this might go to the cops for all we know. Or worse, this could just – just like – bring God and vengeance and Bible kind of things down on us. You better start praying, man."

George collapsed to his knees in the grass, curling into a semi-upright fetal position. Eric got on one knee next to him and put a hand on his back.

"What should I do?" asked George. "C'mon, you're the smartest kid in class. Help me."

"Find a priest is about all I can think of," said Eric. "I mean, I don't even know if there's a word for what you did."

"Will you stop?" cried George. "You're not helping. You're just scaring the crap out of me. If the earth opens up and we all die, I'll know it was all because of me." He wiped at his eyes and nose with his glove, coughing and crying at the same time.

"Let me think," Eric stood again. "Okay, okay. I have an idea."

"Great!" George sat up. "What?"

"First, nothing."

"Nothing?"

"Yeah," Eric sat in the grass facing George. "Nothing. Just give it time and wait, see what happens."

George sat up, nearly eye-to-eye with his best friend. "But what if someone asks me to explain what happened?"

Eric smiled, waited. "Yeah, but what if they don't?" He waited for George to understand, but it took a while.

———————

Hours later, George slowly approached the dinner table. The clinking of silverware on plates, the clunks of iced tea glasses on the table, all seemed amplified as he reached the kitchen.

"What took you so long?" smiled his mother.

"Finishing homework," said George.

"Play any football after school today?" his father asked, reaching to pat the boy's shoulder. George flinched as if he had been zapped by a static shock, but it was barely noticeable.

"N-no, not today. Had to study for a test."

"Good boy," his father said. "What subject?"

"English."

Mom jumped in. "Didn't you just have an English test yesterday?"

George's eyes exploded. "Oh, right. I meant science. Sorry. Must have still been thinking about the

English test." He kept his eyes on his plate and his fork moving while methodically finishing off each item before moving to the next. Chicken, green beans, potatoes, and bread.

I'm being too quiet, he thought. *They might think something's wrong, like maybe I'm sick. Do I usually talk more? I can't remember. Holy crap, I should say something. Anything. I can't just say nothing. They'll get suspicious. Maybe they already know. Maybe they're waiting for me to say the wrong thing. I should keep quiet or I'll say the wrong thing. I got this.*

"Mom," he said, "why is Becca allowed to wear her tutu at dinner but I can't wear my football or baseball uniform?"

His mom stopped with a tray of pork chops hovering over the table. She straightened up, blinking as if she had just sat up in bed in the middle of the night. Then she turned to her husband whose eyes went from his confused wife to his inquisitive son. That's when George knew he should have just kept quiet.

"Something's wrong here," said Dad, sitting back in his chair. George looked up, mouth frozen with food as a small bite of potato fell back on the plate like a passenger abandoning a sinking ship. His eyes popped so wide they hurt. Dad turned and pointed at his son with his fork. "You. You're not right."

"But-" started George.

"You're on the wrong side, Son." His father turned to his right, pointing at George's 8-year old sister. "Becca is usually on my left." Pointing back to his son. "You're usually on my right, closer to the sink so you can help your mom clear the table." Dad leaned forward again. "How'd that happen."

"I got here first," smiled Becca, "and I wanted to sit in George's seat." As his parents focused on the cuteness of Becca's strawberry hair, be-jealous-of-me smile, and the space from a recently fallen tooth, they didn't see George release a tightly held breath. He slumped back in his seat. Not until then did he realize how clean his plate was.

"May I be excused?" he croaked.

"Oh, not yet, Son," said his father. "I barely got to talk to you."

"Sorry, Dad. Homework." He shrugged. "Talk to my teachers and tell them they're giving us too much." George's words caught up to him. "Uhh. Actually no. I mean, it's just tonight I have too much work. I mean, it's not like every night. Just tonight, so no need to talk to my teachers about anything. My bad." He stumbled off his chair and backed away from the table, eyes reluctantly catching everyone else's eyes before leaving the kitchen.

"George," his mother called, the echo through the hallway stopping him momentarily. "Come back here, please." His head sunk as he turned back to the kitchen to face his mother. "I made apple pie. And hot chocolate will be ready as soon as all the plates are cleared. So you better have some with us later, young man."

"Uh huh," he nodded. The smile on his mother's face told him that somehow everything was probably going to be okay. That smile was what drove him to do most of the good things he always did. He shuddered to think how that smile might break when she eventually heard from Mrs. Irwin and found out what he had done at school that day. He took half a step back to his room then stopped. "Can I use the phone?"

His father turned to him. "Calling Eric?"

"Yup. Not sure about something with the homework." He had barely stopped his sentence when he realized that the phone was right there in the kitchen. "Oh, wait. He's just down the block. Can I go over his house instead?"

"I don't know. It's dark out. I'd rather you just call, but not yet. It's dinner time, family time. We don't interrupt family time, Son. Maybe other people do, but we don't."

"Okay. I'll call him later. Thanks." Half step. *Why are they staring at me like that? They're looking at me like I have donkey ears or my nose is growing.* Half step, and he was gone to his room.

That night, instead of sleeping, George was sweating, twisting, rolling, and twitching. He dreamt of something like a crown upon his head, something metal and shiny. He was sitting in a great wooden chair with many people sitting before him, silently watching him. The sun was setting. The sky was a fiery red. The people were faceless, black silhouettes against a red sky. All appeared menacing but peaceful at the same time. One man in a uniform approached him and stood at his side. Lights flickered as George began to feel a numbness, then a floating sensation.

The next morning, minutes after George had left for school, his mother tidied up his room. When she pulled back the covers of his partially made bed, something caught her senses. She frowned while studying the kind of stain she had not seen since her son was in kindergarten

George was scanning the street for Eric and saw his tall friend on the corner across the street. He stepped off the curb, but when his foot touched the street he immediately pulled it back as if he had stepped barefoot into a fire. *After telling a story that isn't true*, he thought, *there's no way I can get caught jaywalking*. He then quickly walked up to the corner, looked both ways, and crossed to where Eric waited.

"So? Anything happen?" Eric asked.

"No." George walked a little faster to keep up with Eric's longer strides.

"Nobody asked nothing?"

"Nope."

"Irwin didn't call your parents?"

"No."

"Absolutely nothing?"

George paused before answering. "Had a bad dream, that's about it."

"What happened?"

"Not sure." But he was very sure. Neither spoke for several blocks, each wondering when the other would offer something. As the silence continued, George felt more alone.

"Your dream have anything to do with what you did?"

"I don't know. I'm just waiting to drop dead or get run over by a truck. Arrested, something. I just know this is going to come back to me," George whined. "I know this isn't over. I just know it. How could I do such a thing? What's wrong with me to even think of something like that? Seriously. It's like, unheard of."

"But nothing's happened?" asked Eric. "You don't feel pain or anything? Cops didn't come to your house last night?"

"No. That's the weird part. Nothing." George kicked at a rock but missed.

"Good. I have an idea," said Eric.

"Cool, what?"

"I can't explain it yet. I want to think it through some more." George's stomach pinched, not happy about the unknown. "Oh, do me a favor. Here, hold this for me." Eric pulled a $5 bill from his pocket and handed it to George. "Don't give it back to me until after school."

As they continued towards school, each breath of the fall air seemed to drop a degree, as if winter were coming more quickly than usual. Scattered clouds crawled across a stark blue sky. They didn't speak again until lunch when George, waiting at his usual table, spotted Eric approaching. He was later than usual with a lunch tray more full than usual.

"Where'd you get all that?" George said salivating.

"You won't believe it," Eric whispered, peering left and right. "I told the lunch lady that I forgot my money and I'd pay her back tomorrow. Then I told her that my friend also forgot his money, so I asked for two lunches so I could bring some to him."

"No way!" George gasped. "She believed you?"

"Duh. Where do you think I got all this food?"

"And you totally made it up, like I did about the homework?"

"Shhh. That's why I gave you my money this morning," Eric said. "Just in case she asked me to check my pockets again. I wanted to see if she'd still give me the food."

"And she did? Wow. Were you scared?"

"More scared than when I lost my baseball glove last summer."

"I remember that. You got a pretty good beating, right?"

"Grounded. It was a brand-new glove I just got for my birthday. Had my name stitched on it and-"

"Wait," said George. "We only have fifteen minutes left for lunch. Let's talk about your glove another time."

"Okay. Hey, what are you doing after school?"

"I dunno. Something going on?"

"Yeah, you're meeting me out front right after dismissal. I got another idea." George's eyes lifted like a dog watching a child inadvertently drop pieces of food on the kitchen floor, waiting to hear Eric's idea. Nothing else was said until the bell rang and they headed to social studies.

The two boys had trouble walking forward as their eyes kept drifting sideways. The store windows on Main Street were getting ready for Christmas, even though Thanksgiving was still weeks away. Workers were busy arranging and rearranging window displays, removing some of the yellow and orange decorations and replacing them with red and green. In another week, a truck would make its way along the curbs, attaching a framework of silver garland, lights, snowflakes, and candles that would create a merry path of light from one end of town to the other. Great, funnel-shaped speakers would be carried to the top of the municipal building to blast Christmas songs by Bing Crosby and Frank Sinatra. Music would bounce across rooftops, through the trees, and dance on front porches throughout town.

"Oh, man," said George. "Look at that bike! Those chrome wheels and the high handlebars. It's like a motorcycle!"

"It's called the Apple Krate. Looks like a fire engine color," said Eric. "Comes in yellow, silver, green, and orange."

George stepped closer, peering at the beautiful bike in the window. "Schwinn? That's a weird name."

"I don't care if they call it Pile of Crap. I want one," said Eric. "And if this plan works, I know exactly which one I'm going to get one."

They continued another two blocks until they reached the same park in which George had cried to Eric the previous day. Then it was Eric's turn to look around to be sure they were safe.

"Here's the plan. We go into the candy store back there. We tell Mr. Cord that we forgot our money, but we really need sodas. Then we see if he lets us take some."

"No," said George, "that's no good."

"Why not?"

"He knows us. And if he ever sees us again, he's going to ask us about the money."

"Yeah, you're right," said Eric. "Okay, let's go over to Hood Falls. Nobody will know us there."

"Hood Falls?" said George.

"Really? It's the next town over. Haven't you ever left town before?"

"I don't know." George felt small. "I don't think so."

"Time for you to go somewhere new," said Eric. "C'mon."

Thirty minutes later they passed a playground as they cut through an apartment complex only a two-minute walk from the edge of Edenton. Their quick pace slowed to a stop as they approached two bicycles resting in the shade of a tree. Half of its leaves were on the ground while the other half were still golden, hanging on the branches above like sleeping bats waiting for dark. Or, near dark.

"What do you think?" said Eric.

"About what?"

"These bikes."

"What about them?"

"What if we took them to ride to Hood Falls?"

"They're not ours," said George. "Are you nuts? I'm in enough trouble already."

"You're not in any trouble."

"Not yet, but I *will* be when someone figures out what I did."

"We can bring them back."

George looked around, up at the apartment windows that reflected the afternoon sky, slightly less blue, slightly more gray. "You promise we'll bring them back?"

"Of course," Eric smiled. "You pick. Blue or yellow."

George hesitantly straddled the blue one and started pedaling as Eric followed suit. They did not get far before two smaller boys were running towards them from the opposite side of the street.

"Hey!" one yelled. "Those are our bikes!" George skidded to a stop as Eric slowly rode circles around the younger boys.

"No they're not," said Eric, bringing a troubled stare from George. *What's wrong with you?* George thought. *You're making it worse! We don't know what might happen!*

"Yes they are. Did you find them over by the playground?" The boy pointed back from where George and Eric had ridden.

"No. These are ours," said Eric. George said nothing, but his twitching eyes followed his partner, who was still circling the two smaller boys.

"Mine is yellow and has that same basket. I'm sure that's my bike."

"No it's not," said Eric. "I have the same bike and basket. I got them for my birthday."

"Really?"

"Yup. Swear." Eric peeked at George, who then turned away. "I bet if you go back to the playground, you'll find your bikes waiting there."

"Wow, that's amazing that we would have the exact same bike and basket," said one of the smaller boys. "I'm sorry about the mistake. I hope you can forgive me."

"No problem," said Eric.

Two smaller boys walked back to the playground as two taller ones pedaled away.

They rode on, following the main drag mostly in silence and George pedaling as if pulling a heavy trailer.

"Do you realize what we can do?" said Eric.

"Yeah, but I'm not sure I like it."

"You can tell your parents you got straight A's in school. You can tell Mrs. Irwin that she was wrong and you were right when she marks your test. Or you can tell the Little League umpire you were safe when he calls you out." George pedaled mostly silently, just following where the road was taking them, his expression very different from that of Eric.

As the wheels continued turning, the boys did not notice the setting sun or crossing two sets of train tracks. Nor did they notice the change from single-family homes to worn, brick apartment buildings, and then back to single-family homes again. These houses were larger than the houses from the very pleasant homes of their own middle-American town of Edenton. Castles compared to their cottages. They had ridden well beyond Hood Falls into a town of which they didn't even know the name, never having anywhere near that distance before, but they did not notice until they parked the bikes in front of a convenience store.

"Where are we?" George asked.

"No idea. Let's just go in, get something, and start riding back. We never left Main Street, so we'll just head straight back." George searched for and found a street sign.

"That doesn't say Main Street. It's," he squinted, "something boulevard. I can't see it."

"Doesn't matter," argued Eric. "It's the same road. C'mon. I'm hungry."

They entered as they would any other store, looked around for what they wanted, soda, pretzels, and approached the man at the cash register. George remained off to the side as Eric handled business.

"Hi, Sir. We forgot our money, and I called my father. He'll be here in about five minutes, but we're starving after a long bike ride. Can we just take this stuff outside and then we'll come back in with the money when my dad gets here?"

The man smiled and spoke in an accent that Eric did not expect. "Sure. I will be here. Come back in when you have the money."

"Thanks." Eric turned with his own smile and jabbed an elbow at George as he headed for the door. The bell over the door rang as they exited, though they didn't recall it ringing on their way in. In their haste and the glory of their spoils, they didn't notice something significant.

"Hey!" said George, wiping a sleeve of his jacket across his mouth, "the bikes! They're gone?"

"How can they be gone?" whimpered George. "They're not ours. We have to bring them back to those kids." His head hung back as his shoulders dropped. "This is getting worse every minute. What do we do?" He turned back towards the store to see the man who gave them the snacks standing at the door, arms folded but holding an awkward smile.

"Maybe we can catch a bus?" Eric zipped up his jacket, which was no longer thick enough for the cold that arrived after sunset.

"We don't have money for the bus," said George, unable to look away from the man inside the glass door.

Eric started walking. "We don't need money, remember? And we know which way to go. Back that way. Let's just start walking until we figure something out."

"Maybe we can ask someone in the store to give us some money," said Eric. "Just keep walking for now, and if you see another one, we'll go in."

It was only minutes away from full dark when they came upon a sign. "Hood Falls five miles. Edenton ten miles," said George. "Holy crap, did we really ride that far?"

"Guess so," said Eric. "Let's just keep going." They did, and they eventually walked alongside a park similar to the one in center of Edenton, the park where they created their secrets and plans. A cascade of trees greeted them as they walked further, surrounded by only green above and the road below until the road was interrupted by the lights of a long, black car that slowed to a stop next to them. The driver clicked off the headlights.

"Boys," said a voice from a shadow inside. "You're out kind of late."

They turned with lifted hearts and stepped forward. "Somebody took our bikes, and we have a long walk home."

"Took your bikes? Why, that's horrible for someone to do such a wrong thing," said the man in dark glasses, even at night. "Would you like a ride home?"

"Oh, wow. Really?" said George.

"Sure. Get in the back." They did, closed the door, and the car moved ahead. "Where you going?"

"Edenton," said George. "Do you know where it is?"

"Of course," said the man, and again the boys' hearts lifted.

"I live on Border Street," said Eric.

"I know exactly where that is." The smiling man closed all the windows.

"Really? Wow," said Eric. "See," he turned to George. "It's all going to be fine."

"Relax, boys," the man said. "And I know a shortcut to get you there fast. Get you there safe and sound. As soon as possible. Trust me."

Long after dark, George had only limped halfway up the seven steps leading to his front door when that door slowly opened to reveal his father. The narrowed eyes, tight lips, and wrinkled brow were familiar neither to the boy nor the man standing there. There had never been a day or a reason for anyone in their home, anyone in town to do anything other than smile the same way one might when handed a slice of toasted bread topped with melted butter. George focused on his father's face and was about to open his mouth when his father spoke first.

"George," in a heavy tone, "I talked to your teacher today, Mrs. Irwin." Inhale, then exhale. Then in. "She asked me how the dog was doing." George's father watched as his boy's face began to mimic the sadness of his own. "She told me that you had missed your homework because you and I were chasing the dog after he had run away."

George's shoulders dropped as his father gazed up, then back down at his son again, leaning on the railing on the brick steps that guided their family in and out of their home since even before any of them could remember. But the boy wasn't just leaning. George Senior watched as his boy hid his face on the other side of the wrought-iron bars. With a cocked, curious eye he saw the boy's body began to shudder, then fall to one knee until his hand kept fast to the rail. George Senior dropped quickly to catch his boy and help him upright.

"Hey, you okay?" His heavy tone was lighter. "What's wrong?"

With nothing but cries, then sobs, the boy hugged his way to his father's midsection before the man hoisted him up like a husband carrying his wife across the threshold of their new life. Once inside, George Senior kicked the front door closed with the back of his right foot and carried the boy to his own bedroom. It wasn't until he removed the boy's light jacket that he noticed the hood was partially torn but still hanging on. It wasn't until he carefully placed the semi-conscious boy into his bed that he noticed he was without shoes, wearing only socks.

"I'm sorry," the boy whimpered. "Sorry, Dad." George Senior pulled soft, cotton pajamas from the boy's dresser. He took an extra second to look at the blue and red football helmets printed on them.

"For what, Son? I don't know what you mean." The boy drowsily extended limp arms and legs as his father helped him change out of his clothes. "You mean about school? What you told your teacher?" The boy nodded between sniffles. "Son, you have to explain it to me. You told your teacher that we were out trying to find the dog, but that was not what happened. I don't understand, George. Why? Why would you do that? What would ever make you think to say something that wasn't – wasn't what really – what really happened? What am I supposed to do now? How am I supposed to understand? Son, you've just, you've just ruined everything. If tomorrow you tell me it's Friday, how can I be sure?"

Tears flowed. Sobs escaped. Arms held fast. But after the boy explained about the teacher and the dog, he looked up at his father's eyes. "But Dad, something else happened too."

"What do you mean?"

The father rubbed at the back of his neck while looking away at his son's room, not as neat as usual, and his most recent pile of clothes on the floor nearby. Although it was dark, he studied a little closer at what seemed like a stain in the boy's underwear. His first thought was it seemed like blood.

"Me and Eric. We went over to the next town. We went over to Hood Falls."

"Hood Falls?" The father backed away. "Haven't I told you never to leave town?" He rubbed his palms against his eyes and cheeks, down across his jaw. "Why did you go there?"

"Dad, I swear, it wasn't my idea." His eyes were pleading as strongly as his words. "It was Eric's idea. Really."

"Swear?" The father began to cry. "Son, before today, the word 'believe' didn't matter at all. If you said something happened, well, then something happened.

That's just the way it's always been around here. But after what happened in school, how can I believe you? You told your teacher, a school teacher, something that wasn't – right. Then you leave town and go over to Hood Falls, of all places. Now I have to wonder if you're really my son. Do you know what that feels like?"

George wiped at his eyes with the both sleeves of his pajamas. "Dad, please listen. Please. There's something else." Through tears and sobs, the boy told detail after detail about the man in the car. His father said nothing, just listened, his eyes widening, wincing with each step, and his own tears pulsing down his face. When the boy was finished, his father's eyes were nearly washed from his own face as he stood, turned, and walked from the room. He glanced back as he closed the door, then he retreated to the comfort of his own bed.

George Senior bolted upright in the dark, startling his wife enough that she asked, "Hey, are you okay?"

"Yeah, I'm good." A glance at the clock showed it was nearly 3 in the morning.

"Are you sure?" she whispered. "That's the third time tonight. What's wrong, Honey?" She touched his shoulder as he rubbed at his eyes before glancing at the clock exactly as the red, digital numerals changed to midnight.

"George told me something about when he was lost that's bothering me."

"What?"

"He said something about the guy who gave him a ride."

"Such a nice man to give a ride to a boy he doesn't even know." She reached to pull him closer just as he was moving away. "I hope he knows how lucky he was."

"Yeah," the father turned, putting his feet to the floor. "But the whole story bothers me a little bit." He stood, several times opening his mouth to tell more but fearing how his wife would react to the pieces that didn't seem to fit. Midnight and a new moon kept his face and words hidden. She couldn't see his jaw tight and his teeth fighting to save her from what their son had said, but she also couldn't see the doubt in her husband's head. *The boy made up a story about the dog and his homework just to stay out of trouble at school. Wouldn't he also make up a story about a man in a dark car, doing dark things, to stay out of trouble at home?*

"How lucky he was. Yes, Honey." The father stood. "Such a nice man. I should find him. So I could talk to him. About what he did." George senior found his jeans on his closet floor.

He drove slowly, his station wagon coming almost to a stop as his car tires rumbled across the tracks that separated Hood Falls from Edenton, a place he rarely left unless he had to in forty years. The silence that continued after crossing the tracks didn't feel the same as the silence when had approached. It was somehow quieter, like when he had played hide-and-seek as a kid, hiding in the basement, waiting to be found, his heartbeat in his ears and fingertips.

As he drove further, he was surprised to see so many people on the streets so far after midnight, but unlike Edenton, they didn't wave as he drove by. Colors caught his eye, a blinking in blue and red neon lines forming a six-foot tall outline of a bottle above a door that opened again as quickly as it closed. Parked a short distance from the colorful sign was a black car with dark windows. He remembered what his son had said. "Dressed like the detectives on TV but everything was black. Coat, shirt, pants, shoes. Dark sunglasses."

He found a parking lot around the corner, then walked back to the door beneath the neon sign. A chill pushed him to tighten his jacket collar. He smiled as he waited and watched those coming and going. The laughter lightened the shadow he felt around him, but he watched more closely, noticing that so many of them were having trouble walking. He glanced up at the streetlight that shone down on him with a cone of light that might take an effort to walk through, like leaving your home on a rainy day. He waited for the door to stop for a few seconds before entering.

Inside was darker than outside, and he could only see silhouettes of people gathered around the bar in the middle of the room, others at tables, others standing in corners. The talking was incessant, like a freight train rumbling through town that never seemed to end. He couldn't see glasses or bottles, but he could hear the sharp, staccato clinks like someone was using them to tap out Morse code. There was a little more light in the center, around the bar, and faces seemed a little clearer, but only a little. He saw a smiling bartender laughing with anyone who wanted him. *Like the detectives on TV but in all black.* He saw an empty bar stool and filled it, but the bartender had strolled around to people on the other side.

He heard her before he saw her, solid steps, like someone knocking at a door. Two or three steps. "Would you like some company?" He wanted to see whose voice it was, but his eyes hadn't yet adjusted enough to the darkness. Two more steps. "You with anybody?" There was a sweetness that he had never heard, sincerity mixed with hope and sadness, like someone you wanted to comfort. The steps grew closer, the voice clearer. He turned his head enough to see hair longer and fuller than he'd ever known except in the movies. Light from the bar caught her teeth enough that he could watch her mouth move at the man next to him. "You by yourself?" George thought it rude how the man ignored her so easily, completely. He watched again, still only able to see her crimson lips and white teeth. "Want a date?" After this man also ignored her, she moved on.

He felt a hand on his back, petting him like he was a cat. "You alone?" He twitched as her worn hands slowly turned his bar stool. She came into full view as she guided him to face her. His hands were still deep in his jacket pockets until he pulled them out and placed them on his lap. He noticed her expression change from a great smile to something of concern.

"Aww," she said, feeling his shoulders, "why so tense?" As she slid her hands across his shoulders again, they melted. She pulled herself closer, forcing her hips between his knees. As she drew closer, he could see the buttons that had not been fastened halfway down the front of her black blouse.

"I," he tried. "I'm. I'm looking for someone."

Her smile returned, bigger than before, bigger but different, and she slid her hands further down his arms and gripping his waist. He watched her eyes as they watched him. It was a staring contest he wanted to lose but couldn't.

Her tongue slid across her teeth.

"You married?" She waited. He held his breath.

"No."

7. The Hitchhiker

*This is a "cat and mouse" story. What is
not clear, of course, is who is the cat and
who is the mouse. Or if either is either.
That's about all I have to say about that.*

"This one, on the right," said a young woman with a mix of dark curls.

"Miss," the Hispanic driver said, "if you're not from around here, you should-"

"Thanks, but I can handle myself."

"You want me to come back later?"

"No." She tossed a $20 and a $10 to the front seat, stepped out of the taxi, shut the door, and knocked on the side of the car. She crunched along the gravel parking lot until she reached the sidewalk that surrounded Jonesy's Bar, somewhere along Route 40, somewhere in the darker parts of Atlantic County. Once on more stable ground, she swapped her low-cut Chuck Taylor's for a pair of black platforms that pumped her up another four inches. She reached for the door but quickly pulled her hand out of the way as it swung out towards her.

"Hey, cutie," slurred a man who had several too many, but she was gone before he could finish the only two intelligible words he would say before waking up in a holding cell the next morning. Once inside, she took inventory.

Two pool tables to the right with a few worn out bumpers. A square bar with about ten stools on each side. Restrooms in the diagonal opposite corner from the door. Kitchen straight ahead beyond the pool tables. One bartender barely out of high school, a couple in their thirties with their legs up on each other's stool and unable to keep their hands off each other, three middle-aged rednecks towards the rest rooms, and an elderly couple near the kitchen. Slow night, she thought. *Not sure if that is good or bad.*

She turned left along the bar and the affectionate couple, turned right past the three "rednecks," and headed straight for the restroom. A minute later she emerged and headed for a bar stool closer to where she entered and sat in the middle of an unpopulated side of the square. The bartender approached and dropped a shot glass, upside down, in front of her.

"What's that for?" she asked, but she knew.

"Means someone is buying you a drink." He smiled, and it seemed to embarrass him to explain it.

"Really? Who?"

"Sorry. Sometimes it's anonymous. It's a coward's way of approaching you, but please don't tell anyone I said that."

"Course not," she smiled, this time because his eyes found the cleavage she worked so hard to re-tape while in the restroom. Her eyes followed his butt as he made his rounds, replaced empty bottles with full ones, and took an order for a cheeseburger before he returned to her corner of the bar. He miscalculated as he reached for the upside down shot glass, knocking it over towards her. As she easily scooped it up, he noticed that she'd undone one extra button while he was gone.

"S-sorry about that, miss," he said. "I was going to ask if you knew what drink you wanted."

"Hmm. Don't most bartenders have certain things they make really well?"

"Well, yeah, in certain kinds of bars," he said, "but I'm new at this. Around here, people just either get shots or beer." He looked back to his right at the three men in flannel shirts leaning together to talk while watching him. "But we have a book of drink recipes if you want to look."

She too glanced at the men across the bar, peering through the dark curls that hung across her eyes. She eased her chair a little left so that her slightly open shirt was aimed at the three men whose poorly trimmed beards made them look more like goats. She watched further as one reached down below the bar, and she imagined that he might be adjusting himself.

"You have a Yaeger machine," she said. "I'll take a shot of that." She watched the three men across the bar as they watched the bartender fetch a cold shot of Yaeger. Two smiled and elbowed each other while one fumbled with his money on the bar. Their flannel shirts that seemed to match, but her eyes might have been fooled by the poor lighting. They also had well-worn Philadelphia Phillies hats that were likely as old as her.

He returned while swirling a reddish-brown, syrupy liquid in a frozen rocks glass, about halfway between a shot and a pint glass.

"That's more than just one shot," she said.

"I'm feeling generous," he explained. "If you don't mind me asking," he paused, "you from around here?"

"I don't mind at all, but why do you ask? And before I answer, what's your name?"

"Devon," he said, looking away and blushing like a slapped ass as she took a small sip of the Yaeger.

"Devon," she repeated. "I'm Elza."

"Elza?"

"They left out the 'I' on my birth certificate, so I just have fun with it. And no, I'm not from around here, but why do you ask?"

"Because you don't look like you're from around here."

"What's that supposed to mean?"

"I didn't mean nothing bad by it. I'm just asking."

"And I'm just telling." They locked eyes a moment. He watched her finger swirling the dark, thick drink in slow circles. He watched as she licked her finger and glance up at him at the same time. Elza stirred again, then rubbed her fingers together as if she were feeling for a splinter.

"So what's different that I don't look like I'm from around here?"

Devon looked around the bar to see if anyone needed him, then turned back to Elza. "Well, your clothes. Not many women come in here so dressed up. Not local ones anyways. Maybe once in a while on ladies' night there'll be a few who stop in for a couple of cheap beers before heading up to the fancier places by the college where the drinks are twice the price an-"

"And so are the cars in the parking lot."

His head flinched. "How'd you know I was gonna say that?"

"Because I've been in here before."

"Really?" He cocked his head. "I've met you before?"

"No, but I've heard you say it to other people. I guess you just never had a reason to talk to me before."

"I'm sorry, miss. I mean, there's no way I wouldn't have noticed you if you were in here before."

"Don't worry about it. I'm usually in here after work, so my hair's not like this." She reached two hands to pull up a ponytail and twist it up behind her head.

"Oh, okay. Maybe I have seen you here. But why don't you come in like this more often?"

"To be honest," she rolled her eyes, "I had a date, but I don't think he's showing up."

"Well, give him a little more time," he looked away, then back. "Can't imagine someone standing you up on a date. Not unless he's stupid. Or gay."

"That's sweet. Thanks. Hey, can you watch my bag? I need to use the ladies room." She hopped from the bar stool, sipped more of the drink, and strutted away.

Although he had previously kept his eyes in check, they were sinking lower as her shoes clicked to the end of the bar. She glanced back in time to catch him, but the three billy goats gruff made no attempt to hide where their eyes were feasting. All six eyes followed her soft ankles as she slowed just a little when she reached them and continued by. Devon was about to reach into his pocket and adjust something when a bottle cap bounced off his chest.

"Hey, Mary," yelled the middle goat. "When you're done dreaming, bring us another round." All three men laughed as Devon reached into a tub full of bottles on ice and carried three full ones to trade for their three empties. The item, in or near his pocket that he had been about to adjust, was gone.

He picked up the remote for the four large-screen televisions forming a square in the center of Jonesy's Bar and flipped away from a commercial during the Phillies-Dodgers game. After buzzing past a few channels, his attention was caught on local news and a graphic that showed a chalk outline of a body. He increased the volume.

"Authorities are concerned that they might have a serial killer on their hands as another body was found in a wooded stretch of South Jersey. The most recent victim has not been identified, but it appears to be a white female in her 20's. She was found by a hunter who stumbled across her body early this morning. Five of the eight victims so far have been female and three of them male. Also, some of the victims were hitchhiking and likely picked up by the murderer, but others victims were seen stopping to pick up a hitchhiker who may have then murdered the apparent Good Samaritan who stopped to pick them up. Because of that, experts say it is too soon to declare this the work of a serial killer. Although their ages have ranged from their 20's to their 40's, department sources have confirmed that all eight victims had one specific thing in common. All were killed carefully and skillfully with a very large and very sharp knife."

"Hey, asshole! Put the game back on!" yelled one of the goats.

"Calm down, ladies." Devon smirked over his shoulder, raised the remote, and restored the game. He watched from the other side of the bar as Elza walked from the restroom and slowed her pace as she reached the goats. She almost stopped completely and leaned towards them to say something Devon couldn't hear, then she continued.

"Fuck you, bitch!" yelled one of the goats while nearly stumbling off his bar stool, thanks to his poor physical dexterity from years of too much beer and French fries. Elza did not flinch as she turned the corner past the kissing couple and back to her waiting purse that Devon did not watch as carefully as she had asked.

"What was that about?" He kept an eye on the goats.

"Remember when we were kids and we would bring something to school for Show n Tell?"

"Yeah."

"It was something like that." She pulled a cell phone from her purse and flipped some messages.

"Well, they ain't my friends. But if you want me to call the cops or something just say so."

"No, it's fine. I'm a big girl. I can take care of myself."

"I see them in here a few times a week," he continued, "but I don't know their names or anything."

"Really," she tried, "it's okay. Doesn't bother me at all. And if you want, I'll tell you a secret." She wagged a finger for him to move closer. "The reason you don't recognize me is that I'm usually in uniform. I'm training at the police academy over in Rock Harbor."

"Really," he said. "Can I see your badge?"

"Shhh. Don't want those dirtbags to know. And you don't get a badge until you graduate and get a job. I'm only in my first year, but I'm working on a special assignment that might help me graduate with honors."

"Really? What's the assignment?" His eyes widened.

"Can't tell you. Secret kind of stuff."

"Okay." They both smiled like middle school kids about to hear a great secret.

"I know that right now I look like some stupid girly-girl, but watch this." She closed her shirt up to her neck and pulled her hair up behind her head. "See. Now I'm more like a cop, right?"

"Oh, yeah," he nodded. "I see what you mean. So you're kind of like undercover or something."

"You might say that." She smiled proudly.

She released her hair and blouse to "de-uniform" herself. He watched each bouncy curl land almost exactly where it was before. He worked to take his eyes away. She enjoyed that he could not look away as her fingers re-unbuttoned her blouse and gave a slight tug at the collar to display just a little more. She looked down and noticed his hand was adjusting something. She caught his eye, and he looked away uncomfortably. She looked over at the goats who sat silently, nursing their beer bottles, except the one in the middle who drained his and put it on the bar with enough force to startle the bartender.

"Be right back," he muttered. When he returned, she was checking her cell phone again.

"Looks like my date ain't making it," she said. "I'm getting out of here. What do I owe you?"

"Nothing really. Seems someone bought all your drinks for you." He grinned. "What a shame, huh?"

"Not the first time." She zipped her purse and tucked it in her shoulder bag.

"You need a ride?" Devon asked.

"I like cabs."

"I was done ten minutes ago, but I wanted to hang around and talk to you. How about I give you a ride?"

"Sure." They both smiled, and she sat back down a little less steadily with a slightly weaker smile and checked her phone again as she waited. He headed into the kitchen and returned a minute later, followed by an older man who immediately looked at Elza, then patted Devon on the back as he walked towards her. On their way out, she noticed that the goats were watching.

"Nice Camaro," she said as they left the parking lot and headed east on Route 40. "And red is my favorite color."

"Thanks. My dad restored it. It was his in high school until he wrecked it after a graduation party. He fixed it up over the years and gave it to me when I turned 18."

He drove at exactly the speed limit in exactly the middle of the lane as she took note of cross streets and milemarkers. At a red light, she moved her bag from her lap to her right side, between the door and her hip, and reached in. He kept his right eye on her, watching the muscles in her jaw tighten, then settle and relax, her right hand still in her bag.

"How do you know where to go?" Elza asked. "I never told you where I live."

He turned his head to the window as the light went green. He didn't spin wheels but let the tires grip the road slowly before flooring the pedal. "I'm a bartender. You figure it out. You're the cop in training."

"You got my address from my license when you carded me," she said.

"You'll make a great cop, once you graduate." He found a radio station with country music.

She glanced left, watching his left arm reach towards the pocket of his door from where she heard his fingers fumbling for something. She watched, trying not to appear to be watching, as his left shoulder dipped lower when he reached beneath the seat. She watched further when he again ran his fingers through the door pocket and finally had two hands on the steering wheel.

"I'm not going home," she said. "I'm going to my aunt's house. About a mile up here, make a left on Whitemarsh Road."

"Your aunt's house?"

"Well, technically she's my aunt, but she's young enough that she's more like a cousin. We hang out a lot. She's married, but her husband is cool. I think they were too young to get married, but it ain't my business I guess."

She brought her bag up to her lap, looked quickly for something, then put it back to her side. He no longer stayed at exactly the speed limit or exactly in the center of the lane as his attention was spreading to her hidden right arm, now tucked between her right side and the passenger door.

It wasn't easy to spot street signs in the dark because rural, county roads are not well lit, but when her eyes found the sign for Whitemarsh, she waited for his foot to ease off the gas, but it did not happen. Instead, he plowed through the intersection as both her heart and the fingers on her right hand simultaneously tightened.

"That was-"

"I know," he jumped, "I missed your turn. I was looking out for – I mean there's a lot of deer around here, and I was – I thought I saw one. You know, when you see their eyes glowing?" He eased to the side of the road and waited for a truck to clear past before beginning a U-turn. He was about to turn the steering wheel and let off the brake enough to begin rolling into the turn but stopped when he saw her body twisting quickly towards him, more like lunging. Her right hand was coming, bringing something shiny in its grasp. He slammed the brakes, sending her forward against the dashboard. Her ass slid off the seat as her right side hit the glove compartment, as did her right arm. Something flew from her hand up to where the dashboard met the windshield. His eyes popped and his breathing eased when he saw it was her cell phone.

"What the fuck did you do that for?" she snapped.

"I'm so, sorry. I was about to turn, and I – I thought I saw something. Something coming. And I hit the brakes." He reached to help her back to the seat, but she pushed his arm away and flattened herself against the passenger side door. Then she quickly reached down to the floor of the car for whatever had spilled out of her bag.

"I'm really sorry," he offered again.

"Just get me where I'm going please!"

"Well, if you had your seatbelt on you-"

"Forget the fucking seatbelt. Just turn the fuck around and go up Whitemarsh!"

He did. He watched blankly as she stepped out of the car. "I'm really sorry. Can I make it up to you? Can I buy you dinner one night?"

"Thanks but no." She closed the door with a little extra push. Without looking back or saying another word, she climbed the stairs at the Berkeley Commons Building A, heading for the third floor townhouses. She cocked an ear and slowed her pace as he pulled another U-turn and disappeared. She waited, then descended the same steps she had just climbed. Then she turned left and walked back towards Route 40.

Not ten minutes later did a pick-up truck pull over slightly ahead of her as she walked easily in her platforms. The passenger-side window buzzed down, and she turned towards an unfamiliar but happy man who looked almost as happy as she did.

"Miss," he said strongly, "I think you need a ride."

"Sure do," she said as she reached for the door and climbed in. "Car broke down a ways back. So I'm heading home. I'll get it in the morning." She took off the shoes and tucked them into her shoulder bag where they settled next to low cut sneakers.

"Well then you'll need a ride back in the morning, right?"

"I guess so. Nice truck. F-150?"

"Yup."

"Love pick-ups. And blue is my favorite color," she added as she stretched her legs and bare feet up to the dashboard, causing her skirt to expose more, and most of her thighs. It was his turn to smile, and she enjoyed its brightness when it reflected the headlights of an oncoming car.

"You live far?" he asked.

"Kinda, yeah." She guessed him at about her age.

"I'm pretty good with cars, but it's too dark to do anything now. And I don't have my tools with me anyway. Maybe you should just spend the night around here somewhere, and I can look at it in the morning."

"Yeah, maybe that can work," she said.

"There's a motel up the road a few miles, I can drop you off." He waited. "Or you can stay with me if you'd like." He smiled her way again.

"Looking at that ring you're wearing," she said, "I don't know if you should be inviting me to stay with you. Unless she's into that sort of thing."

"To be honest, she's away this week on a work thing, so I'm looking for someone else to keep me warm tonight."

"Ooh, you're one of those bad boys?" she asked. Her eyes found his, and they liked it. "I like bad boys."

"And I like bad girls," he leered.

She reached for her bag and fumbled through it for something. Her cell phone buzzed in her jacket, and she quickly silenced it. Then she returned to her bag to find something else.

Devon stopped in front of the bar stool where sat a woman of about 40. She leaned slightly to her right, but only a propped elbow kept her from leaning further.

"Miss, I think I have to cut you off."

"Miss?" she slurred. "I'm old enough to be your mother, but you're cute enough to not be my son." She smiled in a way that he'd seen before from other women her age. He took her pint glass and rinsed out the faint remains of something that had not completely dissolved. Although she did not see those remains, she was feeling the effects of the amount she unknowingly ingested.

"C'mon," he said. "I'll drive you home. You can get your car in the morning."

A raspy, older voice called from the kitchen. "I thought you left? I'm not paying two bartenders on a slow night."

"Don't worry. I came back because I forgot something." He turned back to the unstable woman. "So, can I get you home safe?"

"You don't know where I live," she said.

"Either you tell me or I take you to my place. You pick."

He helped her to her feet, staying close as she walked unsteadily in the heels that were very steady only an hour ago. He eventually guided her into the same seat that less than an hour ago was occupied by the police officer in training. As the older woman fell into the front seat, Devon's hand happened to catch the bottom of her skirt and pulled it up to expose the bottom half of her ass. It excited him just as much as any ass half her age.

"Oh, you think that's what you're getting from me?" she said.

"I don't have to think. I know."

She reached up and put a hand on the bulge growing in his pants.

"Is that for me?" she purred.

"That and more." He reached down to adjust himself before closing the door and moving to his side of the car. "Where's your car?"

"I had a friend drop me off on her way to a movie. I told her that I would text her for a ride unless something fun happened."

Devon held back his laugh as best he could. "So I guess something fun is happening?"

"Could be." The woman's bleach-blonde hair struck brightly against the black night through the window behind her. She turned his way, black skirt riding up as she folded her left leg up on the seat and stretched her right leg to reach his lap.

He moved her foot to where he could better feel it. "Could be."

The red Camaro came to a red light on Route 40. Taking advantage of the moment, the woman withdrew her leg, put her right hand where her foot had just been resting between his legs, and brought her lips to his neck. He closed his eyes most of the way and reached into his jacket's left pocket to make sure something was still there. Something shiny and sharp.

The light went green, and the red Camaro passed a blue F-150 coming the other way. Inside was a woman also bringing her lips to a man's neck and her right hand between his legs. She too closed her eyes most of the way and reached into her jacket's left pocket to make sure something was still there. Something shiny and sharp.

8. The Bus Stop

*As I wrote earlier, sometimes bad things
happen to good people. Another version is
to say that sometimes good people make bad
choices. But sometimes bad choices are
influenced by the bad circumstances under
which those choices are made.*

Meg sat at the bus stop on Second Street in front of the Ocean Apartments, as she had most every weekday morning for the past two years after dropping out of Atlantic Community College. Although spring was approaching, it wasn't yet time to pack away the winter coat and scarf. George sat to her left and Vinny to her right.

"Relax, Vinny," she said as the round man to her right began to stand. "Next one is yours. That's the 10, but yours is the 68." Vinny relaxed and sat back down, as he did at least once a week for the past two years.

"H-how do you always know th-that?" Vinny asked.

"Because you need glasses and I don't." Quickly, she added, "But we're going to get you some really soon, okay?" He nodded but kept his eyes down at the sidewalk.

"My bus is the 32," said George.

"I'm going to be 32-years old soon," said Vinny.

"No you're not," said George.

"Soon, Vinny, but not yet," said Meg with a slight smile.

"I will be 32-years old before you," said George.

"Well then you're older than me so you're going to die before me," said Vinny.

"Vinny!" Meg interrupted. "That is not nice."

"But it's true," said Vinny.

"No, it's not true, and it's not nice."

"I'm sorry, Meg," said Vinny.

"Say it to George, not me."

"I'm sorry, George."

"I forgive you."

"Meg?" Vinny asked. "How long until my b-bus gets here?

"About two minutes."

Vinny mouthed her answer back to himself. "How do you know that?"

Meg squinted slightly and blinked several times. "Because that's about how long it usually takes for the buses to get to us from the other bus stop up there." She nodded to her right, north, up Second Street.

"Thank you, Meg."

"You're very welcome, Vinny."

Shortly after, Vinny stood and waited as the 68 bus arrived. He boarded and sat as close to the front as he could. As on most days, he waved to Meg and George, and they waved back as the bus pulled away.

"Why do you say his name like that?" asked George, sitting to Meg's left.

"I'm sorry. Can you say that again please?" she asked.

George fixed his glasses with his left hand as he pulled a paperback book from his right jacket pocket.

"As you know, I'm learning to be a writer." George cleared his throat. "It says in my writing guide that if two people are talking, one person does not need to say the other person's name because there are only two people talking. To say Vinny's name is poor dialogue."

Meg smiled wider than she would all that day. "Well, *George*," with a little stress, "do you want to know something from the books *I've* read?"

"Yes I do."

"Do you know the one single word that is everyone's favorite word to hear?"

His eyes searched. "I do not think that is possible. We can not all have the same favorite word."

"We don't," she paused, "but we do."

He searched his thoughts. "I give up."

"Everyone's favorite word is their own name, George." She nodded. "It makes us all feel good when someone says our name. So that's why I'm saying *George* to you and saying Vinny's name to him."

The revelation fell greatly upon him, and he nodded and smiled. "So what you are saying is that you want to say Vinny's name to help Vinny feel good?"

"Yes, George. Just like I'm saying *George* so that you can feel good too."

George reached into his coat to find the blue pen in his shirt pocket, then scribbled something in his writing book before putting the book and pen back in their proper places.

"Hey, George, know what else?" Meg asked.

"No. What?"

"If you're worried about writing style, try to use contractions. It gets boring if you keep saying *you are* instead of *you're* and *can not* instead of *can't*. Mix it up a little."

George smiled. "Ah. But that was not writing. That was just talking to you." He paused. "Meg."

"Aww, George. You said my name," she smiled. "Thanks."

George stood. "Here is my bus. Have a good day, Meg." He smiled, feeling as good as she expected he would feel. George, like Vinny, took a seat where he could see Meg and waved as his bus rolled away.

She waited about another ten minutes for her bus, but there was nobody for her to wave to as it rolled away like the others. It was 8:05 am. If all of the good feeling Meg had experienced thus far were put on a scale against all of the good feeling she would have from 8:05 until returning home at about 7 that evening, the early good feeling would far outweigh the rest of the day.

———————

Meg shielded her eyes as her pupils adjusted to the fluorescent lights on the basement hallway ceiling guiding her to apartment B, for basement, where the superintendent and his wife lived. She hated the basement for two reasons. One, the smell of the oil furnace, and two, it reminded her how she couldn't afford real daycare where her 2-year old son might learn and play with other kids instead of sitting with Mrs. O'Dell all day.

"You late." Meg waited to be invited in and assumed that to be the case when Mrs. O'Dell turned and walked away. Meg followed to her kitchen where 2-year old Orey struggled to reach the Cheerios that rolled to the edges of the highchair tray. He was eleven hours older than when she left him that morning, and she would swear she could see every minute of it on his face. To her, Orey was eleven hours taller and stronger, but not eleven hours happier.

"I'm outta Cheerios," said Mrs. O'Dell. "Extra hour, five bucks."

Meg scrounged through her bag, found twenty-five dollars and worked Orey from his highchair. Mrs. O'Dell opened a new bottle of Old Charter and poured it over what was left of two ice cubes in a glass.

"Thanks, Mrs. O. See you tomorrow." Meg hiked her bag over her shoulder and headed for the door.

"And you might wanna look at his leg. Got some rash going on. I put some cream on it, but I don't know what the hell it is."

"Thanks. I'll look at that when I get upstairs." Meg closed the door and, for a few hours, forgot about everything about apartment B.

———————————————

At about 2 in the morning Meg snapped awake, gaining awareness of where she was, exhaling in relief when she saw Orey asleep on the pillow next to her. He kicked his leg slightly when she lifted the blanket off him to look at the rash Mrs. O'Dell had mentioned. She snapped a picture of it with her cell phone, checked the clarity of the picture, and texted it to her mother before grunting and emotionally punching herself when she realized it was still so early in the morning.

There was an audible rip when she removed an envelope that was stuck to the bottom of the glass that had been sitting on the table next to her bed. She pretended not to notice the blue and red emblem of the credit card company in the upper left corner of the envelope. She softly stepped to the kitchen, staying on her toes as they touched the cold linoleum floor. The glass, with its ring of dried red wine at the bottom, went into the sink where she sprayed a little water into it. The envelope, with a ring ripped where the glass had sat, went into the trash just like a similar, unopened envelope the previous month. The single mother without enough sleep carefully slid back into bed without waking up her son.

———————————

Meg sat at the bus stop as Vinny approached. George was already seated to Meg's left as he would never sit in Vinny's spot. Meg was not fully awake and looked at Vinny through eyes barely open.

"Are you okay?" Vinny asked.

"Vinny," George said. "I can not tell if you are speaking to me or Meg because you did not say a first name. Can you specific?" He tightened his eyes. "Be specific?"

"George," Vinny gruffed, "I know you're going to be a writer-"

"AM a writer."

"I know you am a writer, but we're not writing," continued Vinny. "We're talking. Meg, please tell him we're just talking and we don't have to follow the writing rules." Vinny and George both waited. "Meg?"

Meg had not been listening but instead focused on a police car stopped at the red light in front of them. She watched as the officer ripped up a piece of paper and crumbled it before extending his hand out the driver's side window. Vinny followed Meg's eyes and found the officer just as the car pulled away from the green light, pieces of paper trailing from his hand.

"Meg!" cried Vinny. "Did you see that?"

"Yes, Vinny."

"That policeman littered. That's not right, Meg."

George joined in. "What should we do, Meg and Vinny?"

"We should pick up the paper," said Vinny as he quickly stood.

"No!" shouted Meg. "You could get hurt. I'll get it." She left her bag on the bus stop bench and trotted to the street. There was little traffic, and she easily scooped up fourteen of the sixteen scraps of paper as they settled near the curb. The other two pieces followed an air trail created by the police car and another car that followed. Before she could chase them, Vinny called.

"Meg, this is your bus, Meg."

"No, Vinny," she said settling back down. "That's *your* bus."

"That's *my* bus." Vinny lugged his backpack to the bus, boarded, and waved.

"I am a writer, you know," said George, waving back.

"I know, George."

"I am not finished. I am a writer, you know. That was suspicious."

"What was suspicious?" Meg yawned.

"The police officer dropped the paper out of the police car. Why did he not put it in the trash in the car? Why did he litter, Meg? A police officer knows that littering is wrong. Why would a police officer do something that is wrong, Meg?"

Meg, still fighting to stay upright, had already forgotten about the scraps still clumped in her fist. She looked down and opened her hand.

"I think he's so busy with police work that he forgot," she said.

"That might be right, Meg. But you are a good person, so I know you will put the papers in the trash." George watched as she walked over to the trashcan on the curb, pushed the flap with the back of her hand, and reached partly into the can before returning to her seat. "Thank you, Meg. You are a good person."

"Thanks, George. You are too."

By 2 in the morning, Meg had not yet fallen asleep for more than ten minutes because Orey had not been able to sleep for more than ten minutes. He kept crying and kicking his legs, especially the one with the spreading rash.

She sat up in bed and struggled between having to urinate and not disturbing Orey. Flashing red and blue lights, not uncommon in her neighborhood, danced through her bedroom window before moving on. She thought about her high school science class in which there was something, she wasn't sure, about red light moving at a different speed than blue light, but all she remembered for certain was scratching with red and blue markers and making purple.

She remembered the ball of paper she had picked up that morning at the bus stop and remembered it was in her coat pocket. After another twenty minutes of scattered sleep, Orey had convinced her that he was staying in dreamland for a while. She moved in slow motion out of the bed and fast motion to the bathroom before emerging relieved.

Meg settled into a wingback chair near her bed rather than to risk waking her son. She had slept in the chair before but this time pulled it close to the bed and sort out the scraps of papers that she hid in her pocket all day. She unfolded them and began as if solving a jigsaw puzzle, figuring which were corners, edges, and interior pieces. It took less than a minute for her to solve the puzzle despite the two missing pieces. *Irish Pub Friday 1am.*

Struggling to stay awake, Meg settled her head against the back of the chair and submitted to the night's calling.

"Good morning, Meg," said George as he took his seat to Meg's left at the bus stop.

"Hi."

George started, stopped, again, once more. "Meg, you didn't say my name. You said that you should say a person's name to make them feel good. That's what you said."

"I'm sorry, George." Her eyes were barely open. "I didn't get much sleep last night. Orey's got some kind of rash or something bothering him, and he had trouble sleeping."

"Meg," George whispered. "Look." She did. It was the same police car as the previous day. They both stayed silent until it drove away.

"Meg, I think that it is too bad that you threw away that note because I am sure it was a clue. That officer was up to no good."

"I don't know," she said. "If he was doing something wrong, why would he write a note? You said yourself it could be a clue. That means someone could find it. If he was doing something wrong, he would probably make a phone call or send a text message so nobody would know."

George waited. She watched his facial muscles rolling as he worked for an answer.

"I know!" he said. "I saw on the cable television that the police can take your cell phone and get information from the phone company. That could mean that he was worried about the police taking his cell phone to get information from the phone company." George grinned and nodded towards Meg. "That is why, Meg. That is why."

Meg's eyes picked up on Vinny approaching the bus stop.

"Good morning, Vinny," she said. "You're late."

He rubbed at his eyes while flopping down on the bench to Meg's right.

"I looked at the clock wrong this morning. I think it was seven o'clock, but it looked like one o'clock, so I went back to sleep. Meg, you said you would help me get glasses."

"I know, but you have to find out if your work insurance covers vision."

Vinny waited in thought. "I don't know."

"Do you know your work phone number?" she asked.

"It's in my wallet." Vinny fished for his wallet and pulled a business card from it. "Here's work numbers." He handed the card to Meg.

"Don't worry then. I'll call and find out, and we'll go for glasses soon."

"Did I miss my bus?" Vinny asked.

"Vinny," said George, "even if you miss a bus, there is always another one that will be here."

"I know, but I like the same bus because that driver knows my stop in case I forget. A different driver won't know my stop."

Meg had zoned out for a moment before catching up. "George. Did you see the number on that police car?"

"One-one-two."

"What are you talking about?" asked Vinny.

"Meg wants to know the number of the police car of the police man who littered."

"Why?"

"Obviously she wants to tell the police chief and get the police man in trouble."

"No I don't," she said quickly.

"Then why do you want to know the number of the police car, Meg?" asked George.

"Why do you want to know the number of the police car, Meg?" asked Vinny.

She waited. "I don't want to get anyone in trouble. I just know you really like numbers, George. And I wondered if you noticed the number on the car."

"Of course I noticed the numbers. I always notice numbers."

Vinny jumped in. "I noticed the numbers on the car. It was nine-one-one."

"All policeman cars have nine-one-one on them," said George. "But each car has its own number so you can tell them apart and so the policeman knows which car he is supposed to drive when he goes on policeman patrol that day. That is the number that Meg wanted to know. Right, Meg?"

"Yes, George, but Vinny is right too," she said. "There was a nine-one-one on the car."

"Yeah, George," said Vinny. "I was right too. Thank you, Meg."

"You're welcome, Vinny."

"But I am right, too," said George.

"Yes, George. You're right too."

"Here comes my bus," said Vinny. He hesitated to see if Meg might stop him, and he smiled greatly when she didn't.

"My bus is also arriving too," said George as the 32 bus was right behind the 68.

———————————————

Meg checked her purse again as she walked the basement hall on the way to Mrs. O'Dell's apartment. It took Mrs. O'Dell slightly longer than usual to answer, which had Meg hoping she hadn't fallen asleep again.

"Sorry I'm-" Meg began.

"Orey's asleep on the couch, "Mrs. O'Dell interrupted, smiling a little more than usual. "If you want to leave him, I'll call you when he wakes up."

"Well," Meg watched as Mrs. O'Dell struggle to keep her head still, "that's very nice of you, but I'm sure he'll wake up hungry soon."

"Suit yourself." Mrs. O'Dell followed Meg to the living room where she found Orey wrapped in a blanket on the floor.

"Would you be able to watch him for me Friday night?"

"What time?"

"From about ten until two."

"Two in the morning? That's gonna cost more than the usual if you want me to stay up that late."

"I know."

"Suit yourself," said Mrs. O'Dell as she searched for her glass of Old Charter that she had misplaced three other times that day. "But call me as soon as possible if you change your mind."

"I will."

"Finally got a date?"

Meg paused. "Something like that."

Mrs. O'Dell followed her to the door. "Just be careful. This ain't the bes' neighborhood to be out at two in the morning. 'Specially with that clown on the fifth floor. I woulda had him out of here by now, but the cops are dragging their feet on it. Keep telling me about equal opportunity whatever. Not like I'm denying him a job. Everybody knows he's selling drugs. Just ain't caught him in the act yet. Anyway, just be careful."

"I will, thanks. I'll see you tomorrow morning. And tomorrow night."

That Friday night, Meg entered the Irish Pub shortly after midnight and searched the bar for a seat that faced the door without being too close. None was immediately available, but over the course of a half hour she was able to shift and shift again as seats opened up. By 12:30 she was almost where she wanted to be. At 12:50 the person she had been waiting for entered the bar. He had a baseball cap pulled low. She watched as he moved past the bar and found an open booth towards the back where she sat. He put his back to the rear wall of the bar faced the door, as did Meg.

Okay, she thought. *Now what?*

The *what* entered minutes later – the "clown on the fifth floor." He worked the room, spreading handshakes, back slaps, and smiles like he was the mayor running for re-election. He knew everyone and everyone knew him. Two platinum-capped teeth enhanced an already bright smile, but that didn't annoy her as much as the black baseball cap. *Phillies hats are red, you idiot.*

Meg tried to read his lips, but she gave up when she was certain he was speaking Spanish. She looked right, back to the cop, hoping to see him take action on the clown. Instead, the officer waved him over, and the clown stepped to the back of the bar to the last booth where the officer waited.

George was right, Meg thought. She watched but couldn't hear a thing. The officer had a perfect poker face. He barely spoke, but from her perspective, only able to see the clown's hand motions and jittery right leg, it seemed he was doing all of the talking. The officer did little more than nod occasionally. Meg checked her cell phone a few times and totaled their time at twenty-five minutes. That's when the clown extended his arm for a fist bump, which the officer returned.

The clown slid out of the booth and strolled towards the front door, gathering waves and nods like before. As the front door closed behind the clown, Meg's eyes then settled on the bartender, whose own eyes were also following through the front window as the clown strolled into the darkness. Then the bartender balled up a small towel and slammed it into a trash can before making his rounds for refills. That's when she noticed a pronounced limp and painful smirk each time the bartender pushed off his left leg.

Eventually, he made it around to Meg. "You good?" she asked.

"Huh?"

"Looks like you're in pain. And you didn't look all that happy about that guy who just left." His painful smirk was now aimed at her. Her eyes and hands stuttered. She fumbled for two tens and a five and left them on the bar. She made no further eye contact and spun off the bar stool. She straightened herself, not daring to look back, and headed for the front door, certain that a set of eyes were following her.

Only half a step away from the door, she felt a bump on her left side and a pain on her right. She had forgotten all about the police officer. They had both reached the door at the same time but without seeing the other. His much greater mass tossed her like a bean bag into the door frame just after the bouncer pulled it open for her. Before the officer could attempt to help her or offer an apology, she sprinted into the night.

"What the hell happened to you?" asked Mrs. O'Dell as Meg quickly entered the basement apartment.

"It's nothing."

"Nothing? Looks like nothing punched you in the damn face."

"Me and someone else walked through a doorway at the same time. He was a big guy, and I got knocked into the door. It was an accident, swear."

"Girl, I told you be careful. Didn't-"

"Really, there was nothing I could do about it. This big guy just walked into me and I-"

"And Orey been crying all night. That rash is getting something awful. You best get him to a doctor."

"Oh, I'm really sorry about that," said Meg.

"I called my sister. She a nurse, and when I described it, she said that ain't nothing she know of. Might be something serious. Y'oughta take a day off and get him to a doctor soon as possible. Very warm when you touch it. Gave him some Tylenol, but it didn't seem to help."

"I would love to," said Meg as she found some extra strength to lift Orey from his blankets on the floor, "but I can't afford to miss work. A medical bill would kill me right now. My health coverage is only single, but I'll get family coverage in about a month."

"Then just go to the emergency room like everyone else."

"Maybe I'll do that. Thanks." She turned to leave, then paused. "Can I pay you tomorrow? I just want to get him upstairs."

"Tomorrow, before noon. I'm going shopping."

Meg tried to smile. "I'll be down before noon. Thanks. G'night."

"Mm hmm," grumbled Mrs. O'Dell.

———————————————

Meg kept Orey on her lap for the half hour bus ride home from the emergency room at Ocean Memorial Hospital. Her legs shook so nervously that distracted her son from the rash now spreading to his other leg. Meg studied the box for the prescription lotion, specifically the receipt. She calculated the price as best she could,

- The Bus Stop -

along with other recent purchases, calculated her paycheck, and did her best to fight back the lump in her throat. Mentally, she ripped up a picture of the used car she had hoped to buy. That night Orey slept more peacefully than he had for at least a week, but Meg was quite the opposite.

"Police. What's your emergency?"

"Oh, sorry. No emergency."

"How can I help you, Ma'am?"

"I – um – I saw an officer yesterday morning helping a kid who fell. My kid. And he left before I could thank him or anything. But I noticed his car was number one-one-two. Is there any way-"

"One-one-two? You sure?"

"Yes. One-one-two."

"Officer Brady."

"I'm sorry, what?"

"Officer Brady drives one-one-two weekday mornings. You want me to have him call you?"

"Oh, no, that's not necessary. Can I, like, e-mail or something like that?"

"Go to the city website. Upper left side is a bright blue box, says "Police." Click that. In the bar across the top it says 'Officers.' Click that. You'll get a page with all police staff. It's alphabetical. Look for Officer Paul Brady. Click his name for his e-mail."

"Great. That – that sounds easy. Thanks very much."

"You're welcome."

Meg hung up the library pay phone before stepping outside the building, but she felt an unfamiliar tightness. Without caring who might be near, she exhaled with a slight moan as if limping on a twisted ankle. She backed against the brick building and leaned forward, righted herself, took a deep breath, and spat that breath into the air where a circle of oak trees watched from above her. Roughly a minute later she returned inside to the children's area where she had left Orey and Vinny.

"I. Do. Not. Like. Them. Sam. I. Am." She watched as he pointed at and pronounced each word as carefully as she had taught him. Although Orey was not following the story, it did not dampen the smile Vinny flashed when he learned Meg was watching.

"Great job, Vinny."

"Thank you, Meg. Orey likes when I read to him."

"He sure does. You'll do great when it's time to read to your own child."

"Really?" Vinny chirped. "You think I can be a dad one day?"

"Of course you can be a dad someday."

As Vinny soaked in that thought, he was too distracted to notice how Orey was squirming so much that he fell to the floor with a soft thump before bursting into tears. Meg reached for him half a step too late.

"Orey!" Vinny cried. "Meg, I'm sorry, Meg. I didn't mean it!" Several library staff and patrons turned, saw, and turned away.

"It's okay, Vinny. It's okay." With attention on both boys, Meg held Orey against her while keeping a hand on Vinny's shoulder. He attempted to run, but she gripped him enough to keep him in the chair from which he had been reading to the child. With each hand, each arm around each "boy," she was emotionally and almost physically torn in two.

"It's okay, it's okay," she said as both Vinny and Orey sniffled. "Nobody's hurt. Shh. Shhh." She pulled both of them closer to her for a moment before turning Vinny so she could see his face. "Vinny. Vinny. Look at me. Look at me, Vinny. Now, listen." She paused until she was sure his attention was ready. He wiped at tears with his jacket sleeve and nodded. "Orey doesn't have a dad, Vinny. I need you to help with that. Do you want to help me take care of Orey?"

"Yes. I want to help."

"If you're going to help, then I can't have you crying in front of him because it will make him cry more. Okay?" He nodded.

"I want to help. I do. Can I try again?"

"Of course you can," Meg said, finding another book. "Here's one of his favorites. You do your best with this book while I go use one of the computers. Can you do that?" He nodded. "Thanks, Vinny. You're going to be a good dad someday." He nodded again, more smile and fewer tears.

She stepped away, occasionally glancing back while moving to one of the clipboards hanging outside the door of the computer room. After scribbling what seemed like a name, she took a seat at a computer table.

> *Brady. I know what you did. Not very careful. Irish Pub? Really? Meeting that idiot in public? It's going to cost you $5,000 and nobody finds out anything. This Friday, same place, same time, same booth. I'm sending someone to collect for me because I can't trust you. But you can trust her. I'm telling her she's picking up a birthday present that you owe me. Just hand her a small box with the $5,000 – all hundreds - and let her walk away, nobody will know anything. She's someone I know, doesn't live around here, you'll never see her again. You don't show, you don't give her the box, or if she doesn't make it back safely, then the chief finds out everything. Newspapers too.*

> *Just reply with " OK." If you reply with anything other than "OK," chief finds out everything. Newspapers too. Be smart. Do this right and we both win. See you around the station.*

"Another Friday night out?" said Mrs. O'Dell.

"Yes," Meg said. "I met someone last time, and we're going on a second date."

"Well," smiled Mrs. O'Dell. "It's about time you had some good luck. Wasn't no good luck that brought Orey to your life. I mean, bless the boy's heart, but it didn't help you none having to raise a child on your own like that."

"I know what you mean. It's okay."

"You bring him down at ten like last time, and make sure you bring that lotion. Looks like it's working."

"I will, thanks. And thanks for helping out Friday."

"Mm hmm, but same price as always."

"I know," Meg stumbled. "I meant, like, thanks for being available."

"Not a problem. See you tomorrow."

Before going to bed that Thursday night, Meg pulled a stained envelope with the blue and red credit card logo from the trash. She peeled open the damp paper and studied the numbers. *Five thousand will help. Ten would've helped more. Think, dammit.*

She pulled a notebook and a pen from the nightstand, flipped to a clean page, and clicked the pen. She began, *Dear Mrs. O'Dell. If for some reason…*

After finishing, she tore the page from the notebook, folded the paper, and left it in the middle of her kitchen table and beneath a coffee mug to keep it in place.

———————————

"Girl, you going out like that?" said Mrs. O'Dell, eyes popping wide when she opened the door that Friday night.

"Oh, no, not yet. I'm going back upstairs to get ready, but I still wanted to bring Orey down at ten because I knew you'd be expecting him."

"Okay, but get your ass upstairs and do something with that hair."

Meg smiled. "I will. Going right now. And his lotion is in his bag. Thanks. I'll see you around two."

"Here, wait." Mrs. O'Dell reached into her pocket. "We'll probably both be asleep. Use this key so you can let yourself in without knocking and waking us up."

Meg studied the key. With a different set of eyes, she half-smiled. "Thanks very much. That's very trusting of you."

"Ain't nothing. I just don't want to have to drag my ass up when you start pounding on the door in the middle of the night. Now go fix that hair and get yourself a decent man."

Meg returned to her apartment and carefully locked the door. On a kitchen chair was a shopping bag from which she removed a can of spray tan, temporary hair dye, a black baseball cap, and black workboots.

A woman dressed in all black stood in the shadows across the street from the Irish Pub. Right on time, she saw a bulky, off-duty officer on his way in after shaking hands with the bouncer. She had a cell phone ready as she watched him take an empty booth at the back of the bar. Less than a minute later, the bartender called the officer over to the phone. Less than a minute later, the officer left the Irish Pub and scanned the other side of the street until he found who he was looking for – a figure wearing all black and smoking a cigarette. Jaw tight, he pulled his cell phone from his pocket, sent a quick text message, and headed across the street.

George sat at the bus stop the following Tuesday morning alone, still to the left side of the bench in respect to where Meg would have been. When he heard steps shuffling up the sidewalk behind him, he knew it was not Meg.

"Good morning, George," Vinny said. "Where's Meg?"

"I do not know. She has usually been here by now but today is not here again." George turned. "Hey. When did you get glasses?"

"Meg took me last week," he smiled. "How do I look?"

"Yes. You look very good." George's eyes narrowed. "Meg must be very sick. It has been a while since we saw her. We should go check on her. How do we go check on her?"

"I can see so much now. I can read that sign across the street. I can see the bus numbers on the front. I can see – hey. That's Meg," said Vinny.

"Where?" George looked around.

"No, on that paper." Vinny stood and walked to the telephone pole near the trash can at the curb. He reached up, pulled off a yellow slice of paper, and brought it back to the bus stop. Vinny pointed as he read. "Missing per-son."

Half a block away, a bulky man sat in his car and watched two men at a bus stop. His attention perked up when one man pulled a piece of paper from a telephone poll. His right hand turned the key in the ignition and started the car. Although he didn't know it yet, his left hand held the key to apartment B, where an unsuspecting Mrs. O'Dell fished for more ice cubes.

9. The Breakdown

Not everyone gets what they deserve.
Not everyone deserves what they get.

Just knowing her days in a cramped apartment were almost over gave Melissa a little extra energy, so much that she didn't mind the light rain that began to fall as she stepped to her assigned parking spot. *Just another week*, she thought, *and I'll be parking in a dry garage instead of this stupid, rainy parking lot.* In the three years she had been living in the Forrest Lake apartments, only twice had broken glass punctured one of her tires. She wasn't just moving up from an apartment to a condo. Two more paychecks would be enough to trade in her dad's old car for something new. *This is how careers and lives begin. Then it's just a matter of time before I meet a great guy, a doctor, and then we go from condo to a Victorian to kids to a Jaguar and everything else I want.*

Her navy blue suit jacket swung on the hook attached to the roof in the back seat as she cut the wheel and sped away from the apartment where the air-conditioning worked when it felt like it. It was only thirty-five minutes from there to the office. She had timed her new place at forty-six minutes. Even if it were an hour and forty-six minutes, she still would be moving, and moving up, very soon.

She attached the earpiece to her cell phone before reaching 95 North because it would only be about a minute later that her mother would call. Until then, she searched for a traffic report. Instead, an announcer began, "Widespread flooding is expected across Harrison County today." Until her phone buzzed.

"Hi Mom," Melissa said as she clicked her phone on and the radio off.

"Hi, Dear. You on your way to work?"

Melissa smiled and rolled her eyes. "You call me at the same time every day. So what do *you* think?"

"What's on your schedule for today?"

"Same stuff," she said. "Cleanings, x-rays, probably get bit by a kid. And some old guy will probably put his hand on my butt."

"Are you serious?" gasped her mother.

"Oh yeah. Last week was slow, so I'm due for a few bites and feels this week."

"Then maybe you shouldn't work there anymore."

"Mom. I'm kidding. Relax. You convinced me to get out of my apartment. Let's take one thing at a time. I can't talk now. I'm running late, and I want to hear the traffic. And I don't like to talk when it's raining."

What had been a drizzle was now growing into a steady rain and more.

"Okay," her mother said. "Call me when you get to work so I know you made it."

"Sure. Ring you once. Bye."

"Bye, Dear."

Melissa thought more about the longer drive from what would soon be her new condo. The expressway was quicker, but there was also a toll. County Road 152 was about fifteen minutes longer, but it was free. *Free,* she calculated, *or $1.50 a day, times five days a week,* *times fifty weeks, that's $375 a year. I could skip the tolls, leave early, and that would pay for my coffee and bagel all year."*

Before she could disagree with herself, her engine sputtered and stuttered a few times. Stalling on the I-95 would be rather dangerous because there was no shoulder on this stretch, so she said a small prayer that she'd make it off the highway and to the county road safely.

Melissa loved numbers, and she knew it was exactly nine and three-quarter miles to the office once she exited 95. Seven of those miles were along the thick trees of County Road 152. Every foot of those miles was deer territory. She allowed no radio and took no phone call until she was beyond 152 because all of her attention needed to be on the lookout for "Bambi." Today, however, the needs of her engine outweighed the needs of the wild life.

Halfway across 152, her engine quit. Dad's Toyota came to rest on a grassy strip where not one house was visible. She knew each connecting street, but at the moment she was not near any of them. She was not accustomed to and had no tolerance for a break in her routine.

As she was still guessing whether or not the closest house was either ahead of or behind her, she instead pretended to slap herself in the head. Friends had told her many times that it was beyond necessary to upgrade to a smart phone, but her frugality insisted that her older phone would suffice until her next raise. Had she splurged for the upgrade, she could see herself on a map and know exactly where the closest home or business would be.

She hit the speed dial for work but didn't hear the expected ring. "No signal" was on the screen. She looked at the dense woods on the right and the wall of water now streaming down the windshield, making the trees looked like a Salvador Dali painting. As she turned to the driver's side, she let out a short scream. There was a knock on the glass and a face looking in. She caught her breath, eased her pulse, and tilted her eyes down-left to be sure the door was locked.

"You okay?" asked a dark man in a hat. She didn't panic. She held up her phone.

"I," she choked, "I just called my husband. He'll be here in a few minutes." She watched to see if he had believed her. "Thanks, Sir. Thank you for stopping."

The man's hat was pulled low. Water ran off the brim. He looked left and right, stood, and rubbed his face like someone who had just woken up. "Ok," he said. "Good luck." The rain prevented her from seeing him clearly. She thought she saw facial hair, but he was gone. She reached for a pen in the glove compartment and scribbled on the back of a napkin. "Black male, 200 pounds, red jacket, grayish dirty hat, jeans, brown boots." She peered into the side view mirror. "Limping. Old blue pick up." The old blue pickup moved around her and headed off. She couldn't read the license plate through the downpour, but she was content that she had something helpful for the police if necessary.

Melissa clicked the radio back on and waited for anything to erase the sound of the rain. "And don't forget our news-spotter hotline. Just press star-1-0-6-0 from your cell phone if you see news, traffic, weather, or anything else you think we should know."

She was about to call until she remembered having no signal. As she put her phone down, a white car pulled in front of her and slowly backed up, almost touching her front bumper. Melissa smiled as she peered through the wet windshield at a BMW emblem on the trunk. She smiled more when she dropped her foggy window to reveal a handsome man with an umbrella.

"Need some help, Miss?" he asked with perfect teeth.

"Um. Uh. Help? Y-yes," she fumbled.

"Any idea what's wrong?"

"Wrong?" she said slowly. "No." She knew that the real problem was how to get his phone number without being obvious.

"Pop the hood and I'll take a look," the pretty man said. She fumbled on the floor for the hood latch. She pulled both the trunk and gas tank lid before finally hearing a loud "clack" as the hood jumped up an inch. The man with the umbrella walked to the front of her car and lifted the hood.

She jumped out of the car and dashed to join his shelter, moving as close to him as possible. He looked under the hood at what Melissa interpreted as various sizes of metal and rubber with various degrees of road grime. She watched, impressed as he scanned the engine, occasionally touching parts and wiggling things. She admired him more as he blurted things like "hmmm, okay," and "not sure about that."

The umbrella occasionally moved away from her, but she quickly followed it. He smiled when that happened. Her arms instinctively wrapped across her chest as the rain and cool breezes teased her body. He watched her feeble attempt to cover herself, and the umbrella moved again.

"See this?" he asked, pointing at what appeared to her as a random car part. "Feel how hot that is." She reached as far as she could without putting her skirt against the wet car. When she almost toppled over, his hands were very ready to grab her hips and pull her back his way. The combination of heels and muddy ground put her directly against him, and her embarrassed face looked away from his happy one.

"Oh, I'm sorry," she said, struggling to regain her balance.

Her eyes were so focused on him that she barely heard when he said, "Don't be sorry. I'm not." He studied her face as she adored his. "Lock your car, get your keys. C'mon. I'll give you a ride." She said nothing, just nodded and did as she was told while he glanced around at passing cars.

Less than two miles away, in a far less pretty part of town, a man with a red jacket, grayish dirty hat, wet jeans, and soaked brown boots limped away from his old blue pickup truck. Inside was Jean, his wife of forty years and responsible for the heavenly smell of bacon that greeted him even before he entered their leaky, one-bedroom home. She turned as she did every morning to smile at him as he returned from his overnight shift. Her usual "Welcome home, Honey," was cut short when she did not see his usual smile.

"What's wrong, Carl?" she asked, keeping the spatula over the frying pan so no bacon grease dripped on her foot. He shook off the rain and cold that he had brought with him before giving her a stronger than his usual bear hug. When Carl backed away, she could see something different in his eyes.

"Car was broke down on 152. Young woman all alone. I tried to help her, but I could see she was – kind of - afraid." Jean could not tell if he was crying or just wet from the rain.

"Honey, don't you fret none. You did the best you can. If she didn't want your help, then that's her bad luck." She kissed him on the cheek and removed his dripping hat. Then she kissed him on his shaved head as he bowed it in prayer.

"Lord, I hope you got that girl somewhere safe this morning. I tried. Was all I could do. Amen." Silently, he added to the prayer. *Why was I born looking like this, making people so afraid of me? Why, Lord?*

Carl stabbed a fork into his bacon and eggs but put it all down before taking a bite. Jean watched silently, put her hands together, closed her eyes for a few seconds, then caught him looking at her with pleading eyes.

"I know what you're gonna say, so don't even say it." Jean stood. "I'll get my coat."

Each time the white BMW took another turn, Melissa again thought about how he was not following her directions.

"I'm going to be late," she mildly protested.

He said nothing, but again he gave her his glorious smile.

The old blue pickup truck had been parked for five minutes behind an old Toyota on County Road 152.

Jean watched through the foggy windshield as Carl returned to the truck.

"Door isn't locked," he said.

"So?" Jean asked.

"So why would she leave the car but not lock it?"

Carl put the truck in gear and continued down the road as the rain slowed. Jean studied his face, watched his eyes as she had before.

"What you feeling?" she asked. "You feeling something. What is it?"

"Som'tn ain't right," he said.

The rain picked up, beating on the roof of the truck like horses around a dirt track.

"What's that?" asked Jean, pointing ahead.

"We find out," he said. He slowed the truck and stopped behind another car on the side of the road. The rain had increased greatly since they had left their home but now slowed to almost nothing.

"Stay here," Carl said as he pulled at the rusty door handle and left the truck and Jean again. She watched as he walked toward the white car before them and then squinted as the sun pushed through the clouds and pierced her eyes through the passenger side window.

Carl walked to the driver's side door of the white BMW, tried the door handle, but found it locked. He peered inside but saw nobody. However, there was a splash of color on the passenger side floor. Carl began to walk around the car to peek in from that other side but before he could make it, he was distracted by a sound off the shoulder from the road.

"Hey," called a voice, gaining Carl's attention. It was a handsome man, slightly out of breath, struggling to get through shrubs and tall grass while pulling up the zipper on his pants. "What are you doing?"

Carl cleared his throat. "Just thought you mighta got stuck. Broke down or needed help."

"No, no I'm good," the young man said as he reached the road from the shorter grass. "Just had to take a piss. You know what that's like, right?" The man smiled and patted Carl on his giant bicep through his wet coat.

"Sure do," said Carl. "All the coffee I got in me, I should go m'self."

"Dude, no way. Look at me." The young man stepped back and pointed at the mud and other stains on his clothes. "All this rain, I slid down a hill. Man, I'm a mess. I wouldn't go out there if I was you." The young man watched as Carl's eyes caught on something in the grass behind him. "See that. Somebody lost a shoe doing the same thing. Do yourself a favor and get out of this rain." Another pat on the bicep. "Take it easy, buddy." The young man moved to the driver's side and pulled away hastily.

Carl returned to his truck and started the engine.

"Well?" asked Jean.

"Guy was just peeing in the weeds."

"I heard him," she said. "You were 'bout to pee too. Why didn't you?"

"All muddy. And I wouldn't do that with you out here."

"And that shoe?"

"All muddy, like the man said." Carl put the truck in gear and waited for traffic to clear.

"Carl. Look at that shoe." He did. "Girl that wears that shoe don't go peeing in the grass."

Carl shifted the truck in park, stopped the engine, pulled at the rusty door handle, and left the truck again as Jean mouthed a prayer.

10. Mrs. Rabinski

Unfortunately, this story was born from someone I actually know, and others who know that person were not very happy when they read this. Of course, the person I actually know would never do these things. Hopefully, nobody would do them, but it is still fun to think about the possibilities.

With each compression the EMT delivered to Mrs. Rabinski's chest, she thought again about everything that knocked her to the kitchen floor, eyes closed tightly, one hand clutching her chest and the other reaching up to the ceiling fan that slowly waved at her from above.

"I'm sorry," said Dr. Landis, "but there's really nothing else we can do. There's nothing you did wrong, nothing we or anyone did wrong. There are many mysteries in life, and one of the most mysterious of all is when life seems to be finished."

"How long did you say?" asked Mrs. Rabinski.

"A month, maybe two. Anything beyond that is a blessing. A gift." He closed her folder and gently placed it on the metal table to her right. "You should probably start making arrangements as soon as possible."

"What is there to do?"

He looked straight at her without a smile. "Mrs. Rabinski, you were a nurse for almost fifty years at University Hospital. I'm sure you know what arrangements need to be made, so please don't make me say it. And it wasn't that long ago I told you the same thing for your husband. All the same arrangements. Contact your lawyer, make sure he or she has a copy of your will, make any changes if necessary. But let your daughter know first."

"She really handled everything for my husband," she said. "Not me."

"Then I'm sure she'll know what to do." The doctor stood, circled his desk, and reached a hand to help her out of the worn, leather chair that he had added to his office well before the twenty-five years he had known her. "Your daughter is a good woman."

"Usually," Mrs. Rabinski said. Although he reached for her arm to help her up, she relied instead on her cane and what strength she had left.

"If there's anything I can do, please - "

"I think you've done enough," she said.

"Ma'am. There truly is nothing else I can do."

She stopped and turned towards him blankly. After looking him in the eye long enough for him to wish his phone would ring, she said, "I know there's nothing else you can do. That's why I should have gone to someone else."

As Mrs. Rabinski rode the slow, electric chair lift up to her second floor condo, she listened yet again as her neighbor Rosario's vacuum hummed back and forth across her living room on the opposite side of the wall between units B and C in the Coral building of Renaissance Village.

She reached the top, lifted the chairlift arms, and shuffled across the room. She tossed her cane on the sofa where her husband once spent his whole day before continuing to the kitchen where she found a notepad and pen. Then she shuffled back to the living room and settled into her familiar spot across from the television that showed her few things other than CNN, Fox News, and the Phillies, Eagles, Flyers, and Sixers. She clicked the pen.

1. Chinese delivery boy
2. Rosario
3. Dr. Landis
4. Alexis

She clicked the pen again, sat it on the notepad, then placed them both on the glass table to her right. She removed her hearing aids and dropped them on the note pad before settling for a short nap.

She had a dream, more of a recollection, about being 14-years old and sitting in a classroom full of girls in dresses and boys in slacks and polished shoes. She wrote a note, folded it, and tossed it blindly to the student behind her who read it, folded it, and did the same until a soft yet pervasive giggle filled the room.

"Are we all finished?" asked the young, pretty teacher as she stood from her desk. Greeted only by silence, she stepped around the desk and watched as everyone's head was low and everyone's pencil was moving again. Her new heels clicked, her tapered arms folded, and her admirable legs strode the aisles until she spotted a small piece of paper on the floor near the windows. With ladylike grace, she bent at the knees, eyes and chin up, and then stood with the paper.

Miss Alcott was touching herself in the ladies room when we were at lunch.

Two days and a handful of phone calls later, Miss Alcott began her summer vacation a little earlier than everyone else.

Mrs. Rabinski's long-neglected air conditioner rattled, hummed, and pulled her from sleep. *Rosario is vacuuming again?* She reached for her notepad and reviewed the names. *One month. Two is a gift.* She squinted at the clock, 9:00, then she reached for the phone. After a brief stint on hold, during which her eyes narrowed, she cleared her throat.

"Order for delivery," she said. "A quart of beef and broccoli. Quart of pork lo mein. Quart of won ton soup. Six egg rolls. And extra quart of fried rice." She listened as it was read back to her. "No, six egg rolls." She rolled her eyes. "Yes. 448 Thornwood Place." She clicked the pen a few times. "Twenty minutes?" she repeated. "Thanks very much." She squinted again to see 9:02. She looked at the cane that lay to her left, but instead she gripped the end of the sofa and pulled herself to her feet.

In one of the lower kitchen cabinets she found a large bottle of vegetable oil and placed it on the counter top where it waited until she returned wearing her black coat. *Too early,* she thought. Again, the cane watched as she shuffled to the dining room table and the laptop computer that her daughter Alexis had given her for her birthday last November. The computer's outer casing still showed the crayon scribbles from the two years it belonged to her grandchildren before it was eventually given to their grandmother with a mint green bow, her favorite color.

Mrs. Rabinski had always suspected the main reason Alexis had given her the computer was to avoid the uncomfortable phone calls every night. The awkward silence was growing longer and patience shorter, not just between mother and daughter but for the grandchildren as well. They were only 5-years old, so they didn't know any better when they would whine, "But I don't want to talk to Grandma" when the phone was still too close to their little faces. With the computer, they kept in touch through Facebook. The kids and their mother could more easily tolerate Grandma by typing messages and sharing pictures. It also eased their guilt when they moved across the country and left Grandma alone in her condo. Instead of seeing her grandchildren once a week, she instead saw Estelle the home health aide who shopped for her groceries and helped her shower.

Mrs. Rabinski peeked at the clock, and 9:18 peeked back when she rose from the computer, took the bottle of vegetable oil, and headed for the stairs as the cane again watched disapprovingly from the sofa. The chair carried her down the steps where she turned off the outside light and eased open the door to 454 Thornwood Place. In the middle of the day, the squeaky door was no more than a squirrel rustling a few leaves in a tree. At night, when things you can't see might be watching you, the door was more like a police siren that warned others to get out of the way.

It only took about ten steps for her to move from her home, 454 Thornwood, over to 448, the home of Mr. and Mrs. Williams, currently in Florida. A kitchen towel protected her fingers from the heat as she unscrewed the outside bulb just enough to kill the light shining down on the steps. Then she opened the bottle of vegetable oil and covered the three short steps with it. The cool temperatures of a late Fall evening congealed the oil quickly instead of allowing it to run down the cement steps. The chair lift was still carrying her upstairs when a small car abruptly stopped out front and, without closing the driver's side door, a young man with a heavy bag in each hand hurried towards 448.

Once the ambulance stopped annoying her with its flashing lights, Mrs. Rabinski slept more soundly that Wednesday night than she had in weeks. At 10:25, just before going to sleep, she picked up her notepad and clicked her pen.

1. ~~Chinese delivery boy~~

Rosario next door was born in the Philippine Islands but came to America only two years prior when her husband, an Air Force lieutenant, retired from the military and brought his wife to the States. Unfortunately, the adjustment to living in America was more complicated than expected, and they eventually separated at about the same time Mrs. Rabinski's husband had passed away.

It was not unusual for Rosario to spend an occasional afternoon with Mrs. Rabinski as she sniffled over tea and loneliness. It was also not unusual for Mrs. Rabinski to silently curse Rosario for having such gentle, olive skin and naturally black hair that turned her 55 years into less than 40. So it was no surprise that Lieutenant Jackson was distraught when he finally moved out, with a little assistance from the police after his wife called 911. It was also no surprise when Lieutenant Jackson secretly gave Mrs. Rabinski his phone number and asked her to let him know if there was anything that he should know about, such as men visiting his estranged wife.

It wasn't just Mrs. Rabinski who noticed Rosario's beauty. A few months ago, when the humid summer air turned up the volume on her arthritis, she asked Rosario to drive her to Dr. Landis's office. The volume was also turned up on the old woman's anger as the doctor could not take his eyes off Rosario, and the feeling seemed to flow in both directions. Never in twenty-five years had Mrs. Rabinski seen the man smile so much that she thought his face would break, and she was very willing to break it for him. And never had the man been so eager to schedule her next appointment and even place it earlier than the insurance company would normally allow, provided that she again were escorted by Rosario. It was something Mrs. Rabinski thought about when she reached for the phone.

"Dr. Landis's office."

"This is Mrs. Rabinski. Can I speak to Dr. Landis, please?"

"I'm sorry but he's with a patient right now. Can I take a message?"

"Tell him that I called and need to speak to him right away. I am sure that everyone tells you that, but my case is different, and he knows that."

"And your name is?"

"Mrs. Rabinski."

"I will give him your message as soon as I see him."

"Thank you."

She hung up, checked her alphabetized index cards, and made another phone call.

"Mr. Roth please." She returned the card to its proper place in the box of cards. "Mrs. Rabinski." She closed the box. "Thank you." She looked for the clock that revealed it was 10:06 am. "Hello, David. I want to change my will."

"Again?"

"Have you ever heard of PAWS Farm?"

"The animal place?"

"Yes. They take care of stray and unwanted animals. I want everything I have to be liquidated and given to them."

"Everything?"

"Yes."

"What about Alexis and your grandkids?"

"Everything. PAWS Farm. How soon can you change it?"

"Tomorrow. I'll bring it myself so I can witness you signing it."

"Thank you."

"Mrs. Rabinski, I have to ask, if you don't mind. Why are you doing this?"

She cleared her throat. "I like animals."

He cleared his throat. "I'll call you when I'm on my way."

"Please make it before noon."

"No pro - " but she had hung up before he could finish. Not more than a few seconds later the phone demanded her attention.

"Hello."

"Mrs. Rabinski, it's Dr. Landis. How are you feeling?"

"Do you remember the woman who helped me to your office a few times? The Filipino woman, Rosario?"

"Of course. Is something wrong?"

"Well, you might not know this, but she and her husband are divorced, and she's been asking me about you."

"Really?"

"Yes. But she is shy about it, so she asked me if I would help arrange something."

"Something like what?" She could hear the same smile that she had seen the day he first saw Rosario.

"Something like dinner tonight at seven o'clock." It was Mrs. Rabinski's turn to smile.

"Tonight? That's kind of short notice. I don't know if - "

"Well," she interrupted. "Friday she is taking a trip back to Manila for two weeks, and she just might stay there this time. Maybe you can give her a reason to come back. Or, maybe she might invite you to go with her."

"Well," the doctor paused, "I suppose I could make arrangements. What time did you say?"

"Seven o'clock."

"Is that when I'm picking her up?"

"No. She is too shy to go out anywhere and would like to make dinner for the two of you at her place."

"Her place? That sounds kind of cozy. What's the address?"

"Right next door to me, 452 Thornwood Place."

"At seven?"

"Yes."

"How should I dress?" he asked.

"Dress to impress. And I can't stress this enough. Do NOT be late."

"Well, thank you very - " but she had hung up. She had two more phone calls to make, and again she plucked an index card from the box.

"Hi, Rosario. It's Mrs. Rabinski." She put her glasses down.

"Oh, hello. How are you today?" she said in her best English.

"I am wonderful, dear, and how are you today?"

"I am good, thank you. Is there something you need from the supermarket?"

"Oh, no, but thank you very much for asking," she smiled. "Do you remember when you helped me get to my doctor's visit?"

"Yes."

"And do you remember that very handsome doctor you met?"

"Yes."

"Well, I have a great surprise for you."

One hour and another phone call later, Mrs. Rabinski, this time using the cane, moved to and from the kitchen for a tuna salad sandwich with two slices of tomato, the crust removed, cranberry juice with two ice cubes, and a linen napkin. It was 3:17 when she finished. She set her alarm for 6:30 before lying down for a nap.

As most everything in her life, except her life itself, things happened on time. At 6:30 she was chirped awake by the digital clock next to her sofa where she always napped and occasionally slept all the night when her eyes no longer had the strength to fight the evening. On this evening, however, she had every reason to be wide awake.

"Stupid cane," she said while shuffling to the kitchen. She despised the taste of most frozen dinners, but the fire that almost killed her roughly a year ago was enough for her daughter to unplug the electric oven. Prior to the unplugging, her daughter had turned off the breaker switch for the oven, but eventually Mrs. Rabinski discovered that and turned it back on again. Regardless of how many times she tried, the oven held its ground and refused to let her cook anything again.

After the microwave served up weak turkey and dry mashed potatoes with too much butter, Mrs. Rabinski carried a bag of sour cream and onion potato chips to the dining room from where she could see the parking lot at the front of the building. At 6:55 a polished Mercedes appeared, but the driver stayed put for four minutes. Armed with a thick collection of white daisies, a man strode up the walk and knocked on the door of 452 Thornwood Place. The door opened, closed, and all was good thus far as soft murmurs could be heard through the wall between 452 and 454 Thornwood Place.

Mrs. Rabinski quickly returned to the kitchen to refill her cranberry juice and replace the two melted ice cubes. She killed all lights before shuffling back to the chair where she continued to gaze outside. This close to winter meant each day was a darker a little earlier. By the time 7:30 arrived, another car entered the parking lot. This one was not a polished Mercedes but a dark green Jeep with splashes of mud and stickers of deer and geese on the back windows. It did not park but only passed slowly before disappearing beyond her view.

Mrs. Rabinski pulled her chair slightly closer to the window and waited. Even in the night she could see a dark figure, silent and quick, move up the path and disappear below her window ledge. Although she couldn't see, she knew that the door to 452 was opening, someone was entering, and the door was closing. Less than a minute later, there were raised voices, high-pitched shouts, guttural barks, and one set of solid footsteps leaving hurriedly.

Mrs. Rabinski had placed her phone on the table next to her when she had taken her seat by the window. She thought about calling 911, but only if her door was to suddenly forced open. Voices raised, then lowered, then stopped. When she heard nothing for almost two minutes, she moved back to the sofa, found the television remote, and joined the Philadelphia Phillies in the second inning where they were trailing the St. Louis Cardinals 3-2. At the first commercial it was 7:59. She picked up her notepad and pen.

2.   ~~Rosario~~
3.   ~~Dr. Landis~~

Friday morning at 10:02 am, Mrs. Rabinski's telephone disturbed her while it still sat on the dining room table from the previous night. Feeling well enough to ignore the cane, she rushed more than usual to answer it because retrieving voicemail was too complicated.

"Hello," she huffed.

"Mrs. Rabinski? You okay?"

"I'm fine," she inhaled sharply, "just trying to get to the phone," another breath, "in time. Who is this?"

"David Roth, your attorney," he said. "Did I catch you at a bad time? I have your new will to sign. I'll be there in five minutes."

"No, that's fine," she said, closer to coherence.

"You said before noon, so I - "

"I know what I said," she barked. "Door will be open. Just walk up."

Mrs. Rabinski rode the chair down the steps, unlocked the door, and then rode up again. She had just enough time to change both her clothes and adult undergarments, which she needed for occasional accidents while sleeping. Almost exactly as she emerged from her bedroom, she was greeted by her attorney as he slid carefully around the chair lift at the top of the steps.

"Good morning, Mrs. Rabinski," Mr. Roth said. "Was there some kind of trouble here?"

"What do you mean?" she said, caning her way into the living room.

"There's yellow police crime scene tape around the entrance down there. Somebody get robbed or something?"

"Oh, no, not that I know of." She avoided eye contact and went to the sofa to find her pen. "You're probably busy, so let me sign the will so you can get on your way," she rushed.

Mr. Roth unfolded several cream-colored sheets of paper from a strong envelope and placed them on the glass coffee table. She quickly scribbled her name in three different places and sat back with a smirk.

"I'll have one copy on file and two for you. One you keep here and the other goes in your safety deposit box. After I notarize them of course."

"I'm out of checks at the moment," she said, "so could you please send me a bill?"

"As usual, not a problem." Mr. Roth organized his things, folded everything into a leather case, and moved back to the steps. "Have a happy Friday, Mrs. Rabinski."

"I will." It was her way of showing him the door.

She glanced at the clock, and 10:16 glanced back at her. She found her notepad next to the sofa and click her pen.

4.   ~~Alexis~~

She placed them both down again and headed for the kitchen but did not make it before she was again startled by the telephone.

"Hello," she griped while peering into the refrigerator at what little bacon was left.

"Mrs. Rabinski?"

"Yes."

"This is Dr. Landis's office." The old woman suddenly stood straighter than she had in a week. "We needed to reach you immediately. Something horrible happened."

Mrs. Rabinski tried to conceal a grin, but her solitude made hiding something unnecessary. "Something horrible? Whatever could that be?" The smile spread across her face like butter melting across pancakes still on the griddle.

"Your test results from Dr. Landis got mixed up with another patient. A Mrs. Rabinowitz. Your test was fine. You have well more than only a month to live. We're very sorry for the mix up, but I'm sure you just have to be thrilled that there was a mistake. So please accept our apologies, Mrs. Rabinski." Silence. "Hello? Mrs. Rabinski? Are you there?"

"I. I. Yes, I'm here."

"Are you okay? Did you hear what I said? About the test results?"

"Is Dr. Landis there?" the old woman asked.

"No. And that's odd. He's never late, but he should have been here an hour ago. I've been trying to call him but there's no answer. But the important thing is that your tests are fine and you're as healthy as can be at your age."

Mrs. Rabinski hung up. Less than a deep breath later there was a knock followed by the squeaks of the aluminum storm door as someone pulled it open.

"Hello," came a voice. "Your door is open. Anyone home?"

"Y-yes?" she stammered. "Who is it?" She watched from the opening between the kitchen and living room, wondering who might possibly match the heavy footsteps that climbed the twenty-two steps to her living room. Turning the corner was a man in blue, a silver badge, and a shaved head.

"Are you Mrs. Rabinski?" he asked.

"Yes." She wiped at her open-mouth as saliva escaped from one corner.

"Ma'am, are you aware that there was trouble next door last night?"

"T-trouble?" She felt behind her for the wall as tears blurred her vision.

"Are you okay, ma'am?" said the officer. "You want me to call someone? An ambulance?"

"T-trouble?" she repeated.

"Next door," he said. "There was a murder there last night, and. Ma'am, you don't look well."

"T-trouble?" she backed into the kitchen while holding on to the wall with only a few weak fingers.

"There's an ambulance already here for the woman next door," the officer said, "I can go get one of the EMT's for you."

"Murdered?" she mumbled.

"The woman next door. Her ex-husband beat her up something awful, and she died from the injuries. That's why I'm here, Ma'am. There was a witness, a doctor actually, who said maybe you might know something about it. I have a few questions to ask you, but we can wait until you feel better."

Mrs. Rabinski leaned like a heavyweight fighter after taking a brick to the chin. She wobbled and showed only the whites of her eyes as the officer reached too late, and she landed flat on the floor. Before her head rebounded off the linoleum and came to a rest on the floor, the officer was already halfway down the steps and quickly returned with one of the EMT's from next door.

With each compression the EMT delivered to Mrs. Rabinski's chest, she thought again about everything that knocked her to the kitchen floor, eyes closed tightly, one hand clutching her chest and the other reaching up to the ceiling fan that slowly waved at her from above.

Somewhere, far away, she could hear a faint voice. "Come on, you old bitch. I'm waiting for you." Mrs. Rabinski was not sure who was talking, but there was no doubt that it was a female with a noticeable accent.

From the corner of her fading eye she could see the microwave's clock. It was 10:29, and she did not know which would be better – to live or not live to see 10:30.

11. Boy

There are good people who do good, and that's good. There are good people who do things that are open to interpretation. In some aspects, they do good, but others might think that what they have done is not so good. All depends on which side of the fence you are standing.

The pudgy officer closed the rear door, tapped on the glass, and waved before settling behind the steering wheel of his Martinsville County patrol car. "Dispatch," he said while adjusting his sunglasses, "I got the boy. Gimmie about a half hour and we'll be in."

"Roger that, Sheriff," a voice replied. "Take your time. He's been through a lot."

The sheriff flipped it into drive, slung some gravel, and gained speed on Route 60 south.

"Hey. Boy. You hungry?" the sheriff called through the screen to the backseat. The boy stared catatonically watching the trees go by and trying to remember the last time he had eaten. Maybe it was the day before, or maybe the day before that. He had no grasp of recent time but, since being taken from the house, he was regaining muscle control. There were slight convulsions and involuntary cries. Sometimes he'd even open his mouth, trying to ask for help, but nothing discernable was produced.

At a red light, the sheriff looked back through the screen as the boy's eyes slowly closed. Although sleep was his only good time of day, his dreams were sometimes too close to his reality.

———————————

All he ever wanted to know was what he had done wrong and why the man with the boots used them so often. The boot struck when he was too close to the table. The boot struck when he was asleep at the wrong time. The boot struck when he was either outside or inside too long. The boot struck if he interrupted when the man was watching television. The boy didn't understand and tried to ask, but before he could make more than two sounds, something would happen to make him sorry he opened his mouth.

"Shut up, ya little shit! I'm trying to watch!" The boot knocked the boy to the floor where he landed awkwardly and crawled to another room. The man laughed both at the television, the boy, and the fifth can of beer that bounced off the wall near the boy's head.

———————————

"Boy," said the sheriff, "you look thirsty. Let's git you something." He pulled the car off the highway into the dirt lot of the Dawg Howse, a roadside place he'd been to a hundred times just that year.

"Hey, Arnie," said the girl who drew more customers than the product ever could. "Two dogs and a root beer, right?"

"Make it three, one plain, one root beer, and one water. Soda prob'ly be too much for the boy." He tipped his hat back and leaned his elbows on the wooden shelf outside the service window as the August sun found its way across his chubby cheeks. He left the car running so the boy would stay cool in the air conditioner, something that Arnie was sure the boy had never felt before.

"Where is he?" asked the girl as she handed the sheriff a cardboard tray with three hotdogs, one plain and two with sauerkraut, spicy mustard, and onions.

"Lyin' down," said the sheriff just before taking his first bite.

"What's wrong with him?"

"Somebody was beatin' 'im up."

"Oh, no way," she said. "Can I see 'im?"

"Yeah, but don't wake him."

The girl walked carefully to the car as the sheriff almost tried his best not to gawk at her tight shorts. She was young enough to be his daughter. He thought about how many times he had caught her mother behind the counter of the Dawg Howse after closing and always suspected she might actually be his daughter. But if her mother wasn't going to make an issue of it, then he wasn't either. The girl peeked through the window and watched the boy's heaving chest and short breaths even while asleep.

She turned and half whispered, half mouthed, "I think he's having a bad dream." The sheriff wiped the mustard from his lips with the back of his hand as he strode to the car. He watched as the boy breathed too quickly and his legs twitched. "He's trying to run," she said.

"Don't doubt it," whispered the sheriff. He took half a step back and watched drops of sweat form on the girl's tan neck, exposed because her natural blonde hair was piled in a bun on top of her head, just like her mother always wore it.

He stepped back to his second hot dog as the girl traced a heart on the squad car window. Through the imaginary heart she could see the boy's matted, unkempt hair. She took her place back behind the counter as the sheriff tried again not to look as she leaned forward, much like her mother had. Only her mother knew what she was doing.

"Where's he going?" she asked.

"Belongs to the county now."

"You just took him away from his home?"

"Had to. Boy's been kicked so much I had to carry him out. Could barely walk on his own."

"How can somebody do that? He's so little," she whined.

"He won't be doin' it again," said the sheriff, again wiping mustard off his face.

"Poor thing. You can see his ribs."

"I broke a few."

"Huh?" she asked.

"Nothing."

The sheriff flipped the girl a $10, picked up the third hot dog and cup of water, and headed to the car. He left the plain hot dog near the boy on the back seat and put the water in a cupholder in front of the boy, if he had the strength to reach for it. They hadn't driven more than two miles before the sheriff smiled at the sound of chewing and slurping. His smiled dimmed, only for a few seconds, as an ambulance sped by in the opposite direction.

"Sheriff, this is dispatch," cracked an older woman's voice over the radio.

"What is it?"

"What the hell did you do?" barked the woman.

"Picked the boy up. Stopped to feed him. I'll be at the county office in about ten minutes."

"Then why did I get a 911 from that location?"

"I think the man fell," smiled the sheriff.

"Really? Fell? That's the best you got?"

"Swear to God he fell. We were talking. I told him why I was there. The boy limped out of the bedroom, couldn't even walk straight, one eye swollen so bad he couldn't see. Man yelled at him to get back in the room. Shortly after that, the man fell."

"Fell because you knocked him down?"

"Like I said, he fell."

The sheriff sped down Route 60, slightly more agitated and took it out on the gas pedal. He had lost the calming image of the girl behind the counter.

"Eat up," he called to the back seat. "Never know when it's your last meal." The boy wanted to answer but didn't. He flinched at the sound of the sheriff's voice, then looked back through the window at the trees, houses, trucks, and other colorful sights that he had never seen in all his time living with that man with the boots. Things were different out here, but things were different about him too, both inside and out. The man with the boots always treated him like he was different, especially compared to the other boy in the house. The bigger one.

This boy was very different from the one who was usually called "Kid" by the man with the boots. The boy noticed how his legs didn't grow the same as Kid. He didn't walk the same way and often lagged behind only to get yelled at to "hurry up!" He did not have their coordination, so he was not allowed to eat at the table with the man and the kid. The few times he tried, more food was on the floor than was eaten. Instead, his food was often thrown to him, sometimes thrown *at* him. He didn't get nearly as much food as they did. He believed that if he were given more to eat, he might have grown up like them instead of being so different.

He remembered when Kid first arrived, how he'd waddle around and fall on his bottom. He didn't cry though, because he had that soft wrapping on his bottom. The wrapping that sometimes smelled rather foul but familiar.

The boy had different hands then Kid and couldn't open doors himself, although he tried very hard to learn so the man and Kid didn't have to do it for him. When they talked to him, he tried to listen and understand, to match the words with what they were doing, but it didn't always match because things were different inside his head. He believed he knew what they were telling him to do, but he didn't always get it right. He tried to talk to them as they talked to him, but it just didn't come out right. Usually they either laughed or told him to shut up, but he didn't understand "shut up." If he continued his noises and babbling, he usually felt the boot. In the beginning it was just the man's boot, but eventually the kid joined in.

The boy often looked to the kid for help, hoping they would talk about it. "Hey," he might say. "I know what you're going through. I was like you once, couldn't talk or do anything, but now things are different. Here's what you need to do…" If the kid would just tell him, let him in on the secrets, maybe he could do it and not have to feel the boot. Back when the kid was shorter, they would often play together. When the kid used to read books to him, the boy tried to figure it out so he could read on his own, but those black curves and lines didn't make any sense to him. The kid even asked the man if he could take the boy to school, but the man said, "Hell no." After a while, the boy didn't get any smarter, and the kid stopped trying.

The man and the kid often went places, but the boy was usually locked in the house alone while they were gone. When the boy got older, they left him outside instead where he would huddle on the porch if it was rainy or cold. The boy thought that maybe they didn't trust him around the food because he had occasionally reached for theirs when they weren't looking. The boot struck. He tried to tell them that it wasn't going to happen again, lesson learned, but they didn't seem to believe him. They were happy to see him when they came home, but it didn't last long.

Occasionally they would leave him outside when they would go in. When they did that at night, he would cry and then get the boot. They recently left him outside at night and he cried, but there was no boot because the man and the kid had gone away for a few days. He had gotten his leg stuck in the fence. The neighbors heard him crying and called the sheriff. It was not the first time they called about the boy, but it was definitely the last.

———————————

The sheriff passed the county office and made a phone call before making a detour. His wife was waiting on the porch as he pulled up the driveway, and she was almost at the car before it came to a stop. He held up a finger for her to be quiet as he got out.

"He's asleep," he whispered. She tip-toed to the window and peered in. Her first tear was for the scar where there was no eyebrow. Her second tear was for the empty spaces where teeth were missing. Her third tear came when she thought about the boy they had lost a few years back. She remembered how he would lie on the sofa with her, look up at her teary eyes when they all knew he didn't have many days left.

"Why'd you bring him here?" she asked, clutching her husband's hand.

He glanced over her shoulder, at the street, and around. "I think we should keep him," he whispered as he hugged her. She didn't answer, but her sobs were enough. "It's too hot out here," he said. "I wanna get him inside."

He scooped up the boy carefully and made his way into their home as his wife held the door open for him. The coolness of the shady house startled the boy, and he looked around in wonder.

"I gave him some water, but I think he's still thirsty. Honey, go get him something." She was moving before he finished asking and back before her husband could finish wrapping the boy in a soft blanket on the sofa. They sat on each side of him with comforting hands on his back.

"Dear," she said. "You see this all the time. Why him? Why not any of the others?"

He huffed as he put his hat in its usual corner of the oak coffee table. "You know how I am." He smiled. "I got a thing for beagles."

12 Better Days

This is probably my favorite, maybe second favorite story in the collection. It came to me one day almost exactly as what happens in the story. A man sees an abandoned house, sees something in the window, and is compelled to investigate. For me, I saw an abandoned house, did not see anything in the window, but was compelled to pretend that I did and then write a story about it.

A car that had seen better days pulled to a stop in front of a house that had also seen better days.

"This is where you grandfather lives?" said the friend in the passenger seat.

"Yeah," said Stephen. "Don't worry, this won't take long." Stephen picked up a laptop computer and a spiral bound notebook. In his shirt pocket were two of his favorite blue pens. "My grandfather's cool, but he's old and gets tired easily."

"All right, but we got some graduation parties to get to."

"Relax. Listen to the radio or something."

Stephen tossed the keys to his friend and headed for the creaky steps to a creaky, dark brown house. He knocked twice and opened the door. "Grandpa, it's me, Stephen," he called as he almost closed the door behind him.

"Bring some wood with you," came an answer from a voice weak with age.

Year round, there was almost always a fire going in the fireplace, and even a warm June day was no exception. Stephen put his laptop and notebook down on the table near the door before stepping back to the porch where cords of wood remained dry and neatly stacked. There were separations for oak, pine, and peach wood. Grandpa liked the wintry smell of the pine, the summery smell of the peach, and the oak to keep the fire going long into the night. Stephen knew to bring oak and peach.

Almost everything in Grandpa's house was wooden. No rugs. "Don't trust rugs," Grandpa once said. "They hide things." Most places to sit were wooden with a cushion. Grandpa had made most of those places to sit himself. Although fewer people used those places to sit each year, there was still enough for ten to make a semi circle around his great fireplace. The great fireplace had a floor-to-ceiling stone hearth and an unfinished oak mantle, all built by "The Man" himself. That's how Stephen referred to him when talking to his mother.

"Where are you going?" she would say when he took the car keys.

"Going to see what The Man needs from the supermarket." It was natural for parents to wonder where their kids really were going when they took the keys, but if he said he was "going to see The Man, she had no doubt." Her father - The Man - had been a grandfather, a father, and even more to her Stephen. Today, when he said he was going to see The Man, his mother added one thing. She found paper and an envelope, scribbled a note, and said, "Bring this to him."

When Stephen picked up his laptop and notebook from the table next to his grandfather's front door, he inadvertently left that envelope behind.

The Man was in his rocking chair, closest to the fire even on the last day of spring.

"Here comes The Boy," said The Man.

"Hey, how you feeling?" The Boy leaned down for a hug, pat on the back, and the usual gristly stubble on The Man's cheek.

"Same as yesterday," he said. "Have a seat."

Stephen pulled a rocker with a cushion closer to the fire, parked himself, and opened his laptop. "Mom said you wanted me to write some stuff down for you. This ain't going to be any last will and testament stuff, is it?"

"Nah, nothing like that." The Man paused, eyes on the fireplace for a few moments.

"You okay?" Stephen interrupted.

"Yeah. Yeah, I'm fine. I was just thinking about something. About all those times when you and all the other kids would sit here and ask me to tell you stories."

"Oh yeah," Stephen smiled. "Like when someone would say, 'Hey Grandpa, tell us the story about the watermelon, the orange, and the blueberry.' And then you'd just make something up on the spot." Grandpa looked up with a matching smile as Stephen continued. "I was always amazed at how a whole story spilled out like you'd practiced it all day. And then I'd bring friends over after school, and we'd bug you for an hour with stuff like that. No matter what we came up with, you always had a story. How'd you do that?"

Grandpa scratched at his neck behind the collar of his flannel shirt. "Good stories start with a lesson. A good story isn't just something exciting or fun or scary happening. It should have something you take with it. Like, don't steal, or at least don't get caught stealing. Or, listen to your parents. Something like that. The people and the characters, they're not as important. They can be anybody. But a good story is about what people are thinking, what they do, and why they do it, and sometimes why they shouldn't have done it."

The Boy had his word processor ready with a blank page and a blinking cursor. "Well, if it's not a will, then what am I writing down for you?"

"A story. One that's been in my head for years that I never told anybody, and I need you to write it down and keep it. Make sure of that. It's one that I want you to tell anybody who might want to hear a good story. Maybe even put it in a magazine or something. Or on that website of yours."

"Hey," said The Boy with surprise, "how'd you know I have a website?"

"Because you got a mom who's proud of you. She shows me what you've been writing. I'd like to think that maybe I had something to do with it. Maybe all them stories I made up for all those years, maybe they taught you to make up some of your own."

"No doubt about that," said Stephen. "What's this one about?"

Grandpa was gazing out the window, but he came back. "Before I tell you the story, keep something in mind. Just type it as it comes out. You can clean it up later. But this ain't no story about the chicken and the alligator or the three cans of tuna. Nuh uh."

"Okay, Gramps. Ready when you are."

———————

I was driving to work one day about eighteen years ago, same way to work as I had driven for twenty-five years. I go up Mantua Pike, make a left on Greenwich Road, and take that to Route 295, then up to the city. One day there's a long line of traffic because of some construction. I'm at the red light but further away than normal. I glance over to my right, and I see an abandoned house that I'd never seen before. I've lived in this area fifty years, and I'd never seen that house before. Broken windows, overgrown weeds in the driveway. I could barely see the house through a space in the bushes. Red light changes, I keep going to work, and I kind of forget about it.

Next day, driving to work, same line of traffic, and again I'm looking at the house through the bushes, and I'm thinking, something is in there. Something is calling me to go in that house. As I'm looking at the broken window again, I thought I saw something go by. I don't know if it was a shadow, or a reflection of a cloud in the sky. No idea, but I saw something move. So then I'm thinking for sure, something is calling me to go in that house.

So I waited until I had a day off because I didn't want to go there on a Saturday. Lots of people are driving around, getting things done on Saturday, and there's a supermarket and a Home Depot right up the road. You know where it is. So on a day off, a Thursday I think it was, I go up to the house. I parked in the supermarket up the street and walked back down. I had a camera with me and a half a baseball bat. Just in case. It's up the sleeve of my coat so nobody sees it when I'm going up to the house. Just out of habit I knocked, but of course nobody answered.

I tried the doorknob, but the door was stuck. I put a shoulder into it, and it easily popped open. It wasn't a big house, two bedroom ranch. It was probably a living room where I entered. Straight ahead was the kitchen, and bedrooms off to the left side. I didn't even get around to the rest of the house much because I could see right away that there was a hole in the floor between the kitchen and the living room.

Oh, I had a flashlight too. Just remembered, because I walked up to that hole real careful and shined the light at it. I know it was daytime, but a basement is a basement, and they're all dark even in the day time. I got the light going at the hole in the floor, and I'm walking up carefully because that hole was big enough to swallow a table. I was afraid the edge might not be strong enough to hold me. I did the thing like on ice, when you lay down to distribute your weight, and I crawl up to the edge of the hole to look down.

Almost right away, the light falls right on a human hand. Man's hand. Sticking up from splinters and boards and junk that had fallen down with him. It looked like he was probably standing on the floor when it fell through, so that's what I figure probably killed him. I couldn't see the rest of him, but I knew that I was going down there. I backed up, stood, and found the stairs off the kitchen. I know what I should've done, so don't tell me now. I know I should've gone straight to the cops, but I didn't. Should have. Didn't. Enough said about that.

Anyway, typical basement, paint cans, ladder, tools, all that usual stuff, and barely a shaft of light coming down from the hole above. As I got closer, I could see that there was a big blanket over the body, and either it didn't totally cover him or maybe somehow it fell through with him, and he was fighting to get out from under it. I guess he died before he could uncover himself. I couldn't be sure.

I didn't want to pull that blanket off, but I knew I had to. I pulled it away, trying to take as much of the pieces of wood, I guess the pieces of the floor, with the blanket. The less I had to touch, the better. I eventually cleared everything away, and it was just a guy lying on his back. His arm was reaching up, his eyes were looking up, teeth like he was biting something, and lips tight like he was in pain. I had no idea what happened, but I know that whatever it was, it must have hurt like hell.

His body had not yet started to decompose, so I knew he hadn't been there long. His eyes were glazed over, and bugs had been eating at them a little. His skin was grayish, but it didn't smell like I thought it would. He was wearing black jeans, black boots, a dark kind of coat. It was what you'd wear if you were doing something at night and didn't want to be seen. I know enough about people to know he had a purpose. He was there for a reason, maybe good but probably bad, I don't know. I had gone that far, so I had to know the reason, and there was only one way to find out. I started with his coat pockets and found a knife. Had a folding blade, about four inches long. Sharpest knife I ever held. I scraped it against a board, and you would've thought I was scraping cheese from the way pieces were sliced away.

It wasn't easy, but I then checked his pants pockets. His back pocket had a dark blue bandana. Not sure why, but when I go on planes I always have a couple with me. I once saw a show about survival, and they said to always have a bandana. You can use it to keep the sun off your head, a flag to wave if you're lost, and most important, to tie as a tourniquet if you're bleeding really bad. You can also wrap it around your hand if you have to punch through glass, and off course to wipe away fingerprints.

There was no wallet. That told me he was worried about possibly being identified. He was there for a bad reason probably, and having a driver's license or whatever could be a way to identify him. So, dressed all black, strike one. No identification, strike two. I didn't want to move him too much, but I had to check his back pockets. I found a small scrap of paper with an address on it. My first thought was that this guy was dumb. If I'm up to no good, and I have to go to a certain address, I'm not going to write it down because someone can find it. I can remember one or two, maybe even three addresses easily. So why write it down?

Then I thought more about it, and my guess was that he knew that something bad might happen to him, and maybe this address was a clue to who might have been involved. He knew that the other person might win, and he might lose. So if he knew he might be facing something like he did, like dying, or being killed, then he wanted to leave a way for the cops to know who did it. I put the paper back in his pocket, but I remembered the address easily, and I was planning to look it up as soon as I got home.

When I stood to leave, I looked up at the hole in the ceiling, and someone was standing up there looking down. I start shaking and thinking I should hide, but I knew it was too late. He already saw me. Incredibly tall and covered in a black cape, hood, or robe. Whatever you want to call it. I couldn't see his face, but I knew he was looking at me. The only thing missing was that sharp scythe, but I still knew what it was. It was Death. He stepped forward and slowly dropped, floated into the basement.

I froze, like an animal hoping the predator won't see him. Everything flashed through my mind, you know, that life flashing before your eyes thing. All I could think was that maybe I was the one who fell, and it was my body I was looking at on the floor. I mean, if Death is coming for me, how am I going to die? Is someone coming to kill me but hadn't gotten there yet? I just kept thinking, "Why? How? Who?" Death must have heard me. He looked over at me instead of the guy on the floor and said, "Not you. Him."

Then I realized that the guy on the floor wasn't dead yet, but he was just seconds away from it. I saw a shadow, a ghost or spirit rise out of the man's body. It floated in the air, turned like it was lying on its stomach, and just floated head first into Death's hood. It was like Death just – inhaled him. Then it turned towards me, and my knees wobbled. I don't know how I didn't fall, but I sure wanted to fall, crawl, like a bug, just hide in a dark corner.

I heard his voice. He said, "Not today." And I almost cried. But then he said. "In eighteen years. Eighteen exactly, I will be back." Then my legs gave way, and I fell to the floor. I looked up, kind of dizzy, and watched him. He was fuzzy, out of focus, or my eyes were messed up, and he floated back up to the first floor and was gone.

I passed out. No idea for sure how long I was out, but it was the next day when I woke up. It was so late into the next day that I might have been on that floor almost twenty-four hours. When I walked in the house the next day, everyone was yelling at me, crying, hugging me, and I don't remember any of it. They said I was walking like a zombie. Just went up to my room, got in bed, and went to sleep for almost another twenty-four hours.

For weeks, everyone asked where I was all that time, what happened, but I couldn't tell them. I made up a story about being really drunk and going to a friend's house where I passed out. I told them I was so sick drunk and so embarrassed that I didn't want to tell anyone about it. To this day, I'm still apologizing, and I'm still pretending. I never told anyone the truth ever. Not until today. Right now.

Stephen sat, mouth agape, eyes wide, hands ready and waiting to type more, but that was it. The Man was done with the story. "And?"

"There's no *and*. That's it."

"Are you kidding me?" said Stephen. "That was brilliant! Oh, man. I can really put that on my website? For real?"

"Sure," said The Man. "Do whatever you want with it. Put your own name, if you want. Pretend you wrote it. I don't mind."

"No, Gramps. I'm not taking credit for that. It's your work. It's a great story. I'll clean this up tonight and post it tomorrow. But your name goes on it."

"I'd really prefer if you said it was yours."

"Can't do that, but thanks anyway."

"What if we say it's your birthday present?" his grandfather tried.

"Tempting, but still no," said Stephen. "If that's the end, then I gotta get going. My friend's waiting outside in the car."

They stood and walked together towards the front door, Stephen with his laptop and notebook, and Grandpa leaning on his cane. The boy stepped outside to the porch and turned around for a goodbye hug. Instead, he saw his grandfather's outstretched arm with something shiny in his hand.

"What?" Stephen asked.

"Take it."

"I got Mom's car."

"No, I mean take it. Keep it. It's yours."

"Your car? The Corvette?"

"Birthday present. You're eighteen today. Going to college in two months. You can't keep borrowing your mom's car. Hell, I can't drive anymore. You take it. Please."

Stephen walked back, eyes fixed as well as his smile. He took the keys and held them up as if he were trying to hypnotize himself. "I have to check with Mom first, but this is awesome!" He stepped back, gave The Man a big hug, and ran down the porch steps to his friend, still waiting in his mother's car. He got in, keeping the Corvette keys a secret for the moment, and they drove away.

The Man closed the door but didn't lock it. He noticed the envelope on the table and opened it.

Dear Dad,

Eighteen years ago today your grandson was born. Although you weren't there to see it, thank you for being there every other day ever since.

Thanks, and Love You Too

He trudged back towards the living room where the fire had softened. He leaned his cane on his rocking chair before grabbing a few pieces of oak from the bunch that his grandson had brought in. After dropping them on top of the fire, he returned to his rocking chair. As he stretched, he wasn't sure which crackled more – his legs or the fire. The extra heat reached his right leg and right arm first, then eventually he warmed up all over, but then he dozed off for a while until startled awake as if from a bad dream.

Across from him, in the chair where Stephen had previously sat only about ten minutes before, was a massive figure with a dark hood. No visible face.

"Your fire," it said, "has seen better days."

13. Her Best Feature

I started out writing a story about a womanizer, a guy who can't keep it in his pants. Not that I would know what that was like, but anyway – it morphed into something far better. Something most of us could only dream about, even on our best day. When my friends read this story, most of them didn't like it, but I think they misunderstood it. Let me know if you don't like it, and I will gladly try to change your mind. You know where to reach me.

Jake checked his Rolex as he settled into the sofa across from the doctor. Although her face was blocked by her open notebook, he had a well-enough glimpse of her legs. The right one, always crossed over the left, bounced slightly but never granted his wish of opening far enough for a glimpse of anything that a doctor should not show a patient. What she did give him, unintentionally, was that occasional move of her shoe slipping off her heel, dangling on her toes before she clenched those toes and pulled it back on again. That move had all of his attention.

"So," she said, "this is our," papers ruffled, "tenth visit? And I'm not sure if we're getting anywhere. You still have some issues with sexuality, and – to be quite honest – I feel you're holding back in order to protect yourself." Papers fell back into place. "I have to question what your real purpose is for being here."

Jake had heard every word, but instead of again crafting an answer that sounded like what he knew she wanted to hear, his impatience focused instead on whether or not the crotch of his pants had gathered in just the right way. Without any attempt to be inconspicuous, he again grabbed an eyeful of legs – her best feature - which solved his crotch dilemma.

"Are you listening at all?" she asked.

"Look," he sat up, "Doc, how much longer are we going to continue this song and dance?"

"Not," she checked her next appointment time, then glanced at the clock, "not long."

Jake stood from the leather sofa and strutted to the bank of wall-height windows that overlooked the downtown area. Downtown looked back at what was not just the tallest building on the west side but the most prestigious medical complex in the state. He glanced at other windows, specifically the Hilton, hoping to catch sight of at least one couple engaged in something designed to be "accidentally" seen by those in nearby buildings. Not everyone knew where and when to look, but Jake knew.

After his hand left his pocket, he turned back to the doctor and tried his worst not to direct her eyes below his belt. She, likewise, did not do her best.

"Mr. Gianelli," she cleared her throat, "unless you stay on the couch, and stay more honest, this is going to be a great waste of time and money."

"I got the time," Jake said, "and the money. Maybe if you didn't aim those legs at me like that, we could get somewhere." He removed his jacket and tossed it on the chair behind her mahogany desk. "You know what the cops say. Don't draw your weapon unless you're ready to use it." He smiled, as he often did, in ways that affected her skin.

"Mr. Gianelli, I am not aiming anything at you. Maybe I should make a note to wear pants instead of skirts on days when we are scheduled to meet."

He strolled behind her wingback chair until he was where her neck couldn't turn far enough. He attempted to tug at his zipper slowly enough so that she couldn't hear it, but then he noticed her head turn sharply enough for her earrings to dance. Her hand tightened on her favorite gel pen.

The next day, Jake parked his car in front of the Hilton and tossed his keys to the valet. As his Jaguar disappeared into the garage, a woman's voice greeted his phone call.

"You're late," she said.

"Appointment with my therapist ran late."

"Therapist? For what?"

"Sexual addiction. Like you didn't know. I'm downstairs. You good?"

"Room 520. Door is open."

"What if someone gets there first?"

"You'll have to wait your turn," she purred, "but feel free to watch."

"What if I want to join in?" he said.

"Then I'll have to charge you extra. Just get your balls up here and stop wasting my time. I have a business to run."

On the elevator up to the fifth floor, he recalled how he adored to gather up her strawberry-blonde hair – her best feature - tug her head backwards, and feast on her neck.

When he entered the room, the curtains were open and she was standing , wrapped in a bed sheet before one of the same windows he had searched the previous day but from the building across the street. By the time he made it from the door to the window, he was wearing as little as she was. Once he reached her, he looked up to find one specific office. It was dark, but there was enough of a lunchtime crowd on the sidewalk.

The next day, Jake untied the ropes from the dock before climbing to the flying bridge. He throttled the boat slowly and increased speed as they moved from the marina to the bay.

"Like it?" he asked.

"Love it!" said the woman with the 40 D's testing the strength of her bikini top. She moved closer to him, feeling buzzes both from the mojitos and the dual inboard Evinrudes as they passed beneath the bridge and waved to the people along the rail and waiting for the draw bridge to flatten.

Jake slide his hand down to the low-cut bottoms and then up her oiled back, found the string, and pulled. Her top did not loosen enough to totally uncover her breasts – her best feature - but there was enough visible on her so that there was enough visible on him. His hand slid up her back to her neck where he gripped a little extra before guiding her face to his for a deep kiss. His left hand steered the boat, and her right hand steered him.

As they reached the inlet, he waved to several other watercraft whose captains waved back, paused, and waved again with a smile.

The next day, as Jake held three different ties against his white, dress shirt, his glance was stolen by something in the mirror. He tried again, failed to settle on a tie, but kept them in his fist as he moved like a mouse in a maze through racks of clothing towards a fabulously round ass – her best feature.

"Miss," he whispered. She didn't seem to react. "Do you know how difficult it is to select a tie while you and your perfect ass are walking around the men's department?"

Without turning to see him, she said, "Do you know how difficult it is for me to find a Father's Day shirt for my husband when your equally perfect ass is walking around the same men's department?"

She strutted away, but he followed as she neared the fitting rooms. After a quick survey, he took hold of her collar and tugged her to the right, into an empty fitting room. There, they were mostly out of sight except their intertlocked ankles.

The next day at a dinner party, Jake sat next to an empty chair waiting for yet another eye-rolling conversation about someone's honor student or Caribbean vacation when five delicate fingers, one with a two-carat diamond but all with crimson nails, made their presence known across the back of his head.

"You look bored," she said.

"Just got better. What about you?"

"Eh, my husband dragged me to this. Made me leave the nude beach early." He watched as a sip of wine flowed between soft lips – her best feature – that matched her crimson nails. She mimicked a whiny voice, "These networking parties are what keeps the customers and pay the bills and blah blah blah."

"I know what you mean." Jake finished his straight vodka. "My wife whines a lot too, but what if your husband is right? He knows what he's doing, no denying that."

"Sometimes the alcohol alone costs more than it brings in," she said between sips of wine.

"What if he lands City Cadillac tonight?"

"If he did, I'll meet you in the pool house."

"Be right back." Jake took their empty glasses towards the hired bartender stationed on the patio. Less than a minute later, an elderly man with thick glasses slowly approached the woman with crimson lips.

"Excuse me," the man said, "I have to go, but I wanted to thank you for everything."

"I'm sorry," she said, standing to shake his hand, "but have we met?"

"We have not met, my loss, but we will be seeing each other again, I'm sure. I'm Art Fielder." They clasped hands, but his unsteady hand didn't notice how she flinched when he added, "City Cadillac. Really looking forward to doing business with you and your husband." He pushed up his thick glasses.

"Doing business," she said, jaw slightly tight, while Jake watched from across the room, straight vodka in one hand. Smiling, he sipped from her wine glass in his other hand. Still smiling, he turned and headed out to the pool house where he waited, but not for long.

The next day Jake slowed and parked at an outdoor café near the brownstone section of the city. Although he cut the music before he lowered the windows, enough eyes had already turned. One set of eyes, a cool blue – her best feature – stayed on him after the others had turned back to their lunches, conversations, and cell phones. He nodded in such a way to invite her over. With each step her eyes grew bigger, as did a certain part of Jake.

"Why are you driving an Escalade?"

"You want it?"

"Shut up."

"I'm serious. Pick a color."

"Blue. Who do I have to sleep with to get one?"

"Me."

She stepped back for her purse, left $40 under the sandwich plate, and slid into the passenger seat. Before the door closed, his pants were already unzipped. She returned to the office a little later than usual and with her skirt crooked enough that a few of the other women noticed. It was not the first time. Not even the first time that week.

The next evening, Jake's towel fell as he walked from the grotto shower to the bedroom where his wife, half asleep, was semi watching *Under the Tuscan Sun*, with Diane Lane. He tossed the towel to the floor, killed the lights, and slipped into bed next to her. He ran his left hand behind her smooth left shoulder and carefully pulled her body closer, letting her face settle against his stomach. After teasing himself, he found her left hand and placed it right where he wanted it. For only a moment she peered up, eyes half open, but open enough for her to see he was home and show that wonderful smile – her best feature. Although she seemed not fully conscious, she knew enough to follow his lead. Eventually, they both slept very well.

The next day Jake strolled with glances left and right, each time deciding that no matter what height any particular woman's heels might have been, they should have been one inch higher, skirts "one inch, no, two inches shorter." He slowed when he reached the windows of Gorgeous Nails, hopeful and then happy when he saw someone inside.

Her eyes were closed and had been for long enough to have fallen into a light sleep as a woman with less-than-perfect English was massaging her feet. However, when she awoke, it was Jake massaging the cucumber lotion on her feet – her best feature. Only slightly startled, she closed her eyes and let her head fall back.

Twice in fifteen minutes her breathing and heart rate increased enough to squeak out sounds that did not go unnoticed by the jealous women sitting nearby. After the second shudder, she fell again into a nap, but he was gone by the time she woke up again. She frowned slightly, thinking about when she might see him again.

When she pulled her credit card to pay, the woman at the register said, "Already paid for."

"I'm sorry?" she asked.

"That man who was here. He paid, and he told me to give you this note."

Sorry I couldn't stay. Meeting wife for dinner. I'm sure you understand.

Hours later, Jake stood when a woman in a strapless, black dress entered the restaurant lit only by each table's candles. He thought about taking a bite out of her soft shoulders – her best feature – and he approached. She gave him a disinterested glance, almost placed her purse on an empty table at which a man in a bow tie was holding a chair for her, but veered towards the bar instead.

"Malibu rum on the rocks," she ordered. Jake nodded to the bartender, pointed to himself, and delivered the glass to her.

"Give it a rest, buddy," she said. "I'm meeting someone."

"Me too." He watched as she crossed her legs – her best feature – as they stretched out from beneath her dress. She turned away from him, but he was fixated on her strawberry blonde hair – her best feature – as it landed in bright contrast to the black dress.

"Can we talk until he gets here?" Jake asked.

She turned towards him. "You really think I'm going to say 'yes'?" His face went from serious to a slight grin once he saw her sarcastic smile – her best feature.

He stepped closer and tried his worst not to stare when he realized she had no trouble holding up a strapless dress with what were, to him, perfect breasts – her best feature.

"Really?" She snarled with disgust and hopped from her chair, landing easily on tall, black heels. As she strutted away, he watched the bottom of her dress as it hugged the curve of her ass – her best feature. When she realized he was following, she turned to face him.

"I just want to say hi," Jake whined. Whatever she had said to him, he heard nothing and remained focused on her darkly painted lips – her best feature – before drifting up to her cool blue eyes – her best feature.

He took the drink from her hand, swallowed it, dropped the glass in front of people at a nearby table, and grabbed her hand. "Let's dance." She wasn't ready for that, and struggled to resist. she sensed she might twist an ankle in her tall heels and stepped out of her shoes, staying on the edge of the dance floor in bare feet – her best feature.

Sensing her confused vulnerability, he reached an arm around her waist and pulled her against him, where there was no mistaking how excited he was. She pushed back slightly, only slightly.

"You're one of those guys who thinks he can get every woman he wants."

"Not *every* woman. Only the best."

She stepped back into her heels and strutted back to the table at which she had almost dropped her purse, but now there was a bouquet of twenty-five roses and a silver-framed wedding picture from twenty-five years prior. Leaning against the frame was an envelope on which was written "Happy Anniversary, Mr. and Mrs. Gianelli."

She turned to deliver a kiss to her husband, who then gave a kiss back to his wife – his best feature.

Thanks for reading.

Acknowledgements

Thanks very much to the good people at WordPress, without whom this book would not be as good. Hell, I can't say "not possible," I mean, be real. But WordPress allowed me to share this with beta-readers in order to critique and improve each story a little at a time.

Thanks especially to those WordPress friends in California, Florida, Iowa, Louisiana, Ohio, Canada, England, Israel, Mexico, and other places.

Decker Schutt

I've been writing since 4th grade when I forgot to write a summer book report and made up a book called "Carrot Top Mr. Mouse" about a mouse ridiculed for his red hair, people we now call "gingers."

After accidentally becoming a writing/English teacher for 25 years, I'm taking the writing thing more seriously than I've ever done before. With your help, it should work out well.

Most days I drink coffee and wonder if anyone will read anything I write on www.brainsnorts.com. Some days I just sit on the beach, listen to baseball and watch the waves, with friends and a cooler nearby.

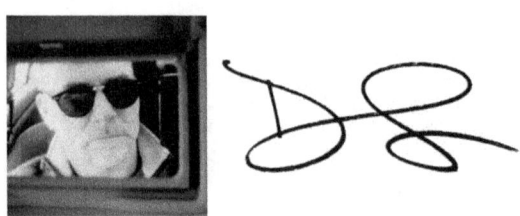

www.ingramcontent.com/pod-product-compliance
Lightning Source LLC
Chambersburg PA
CBHW060142130626
46556CB00006B/2452